Someone Like Her

Brittni Huyck

Rae- You inspire me in more ways than one. This book is just as much your baby as it is mine.

"Stay close to people who feel like sunshine."
-unknown

Prologue

Lenny: I don't know if I can do this Graham.

I stare down at my phone, reading the words that I knew were coming, but silently hoped wouldn't. I've spent the last four years of my life with Lennox Coleman, and I can't imagine spending any of the next one hundred without her. The year she moved to Iron City was the best yet. I'll never forget watching her walk into our gym class halfway through freshman year.

"Everyone, I would like you to meet Lennox Coleman", everything else in that moment drifted away when I looked up and saw her face. The way her chestnut hair sits on top of her head in one of those high ponytails, leaving small pieces out to frame her perfect cheeks and dimples. This girl isn't like any of the others I go to school with, no, she looks real. Her beauty

isn't masked with caked on makeup, nor is she wearing skintight shorts, or a barely there tank top.

Instead, her athletic shorts are showing just enough of her tan, toned legs to keep any straight guy interested, and they're paired with a worn looking Matchbox 20 T-shirt. She clearly has crap taste in music but I suppose if everything else about her is perfect, I can't fault her for that.

"Oh. My. God. What is she wearing?" I glance over to the group of girls sitting beside me, suddenly wondering why I continue to surround myself with them. Chelsea's probably the worst, and lucky for me, she seems to have staked her claim on me - warning all the others to stay away because apparently I'm "hers".

Lennox sits a few feet away by herself, not that I can blame her, the options of friendly faces in this class right now are slim pickings. Besides me, my best friend Jace, and a few of the other guys from the baseball team, the gym's filled with girls who are only here to be close to us.

I stand up and head in the direction of the new girl. "Um, where exactly do you think you're going?" Chelsea snarks as I pass.

"To be a genuinely good human being and introduce myself. Maybe you should try it, you know, being genuine or a good human being?" I smirk, raising an eyebrow on my way by.

She mumbles something under her breath, but I don't care enough to turn and ask her to repeat it. I plop down, closer than what Lennox apparently feels comfortable with because as she turns to look at me she slides a few inches in the opposite direction.

"Hey, I'm Graham."

Her cheeks flush as she subtly looks me up and down. Okay, maybe she isn't so subtle about it, but at least she's controlling herself enough to not obnoxiously gawk like the other girls do. "I'm Lennox, which you already know because the teacher just told you. Sorry, I swear I'm not always this awkward, but this whole being the "new girl" thing sucks. By the way, your girlfriend looks super pissed off that you are over here with me and not by her."

I turn and look up at Chelsea and her group of minions who all seem to be throwing eye daggers our way. I laugh, and I pull my attention back to Lennox, "Oh, Chelsea, she's definitely not my girlfriend."

"Huh. Well, someone should tell her that." She smiles.

Oh, that smile, she could end wars with that smile. Yeah, Lennox Coleman is going to be trouble with a capital T, but I think she's just the right kind of trouble for me.

A slap on my back wakes me out of my memory, "Hey, big bro, where's Lenny? I wanted to show her all of the new clothes I got when mom and I went back to school shopping last week." My little sister, Halee, is only two years younger than me but she's the definition of "baby of the family". There's a reason we all call her princess.

"She should be here soon." My answer seems believable enough that Halee trots away, joining her best friend Quinn over by the bonfire.

Me: Please Len. Don't give up on us yet. I know that me going into the Army isn't ideal, but it's what I've dreamed about since I was a kid. Everything's going to be okay, and we'll

figure out the "us" part along the way. Please, I need you Lenny.

I sit and wait for her reply. I wish they would invent a phone that had a way for you to see when someone has read your text or even better, when they are texting back. But I shouldn't complain too much, I love that we can text now instead of always having to call or chirp people.

My phone vibrates.

Lenny: I love you Graham, but I have so many dreams of my own and none of them include being married to the military. I just need some time and unfortunately, time is something I don't have. You leave tomorrow.

Me: I know you have dreams, and I know how important it is that you follow them and become a big, badass attorney. I have to get on the bus in less than twelve hours, I hope you change your mind and come to the party. I can't imagine doing it without seeing you at least one more time. I love you, Lennox.

I wait a few more minutes with no reply before I pocket my phone and head over to where everyone else is. My parents thought it was important to throw this giant going away party before I left, and at first I was cool with it. But now - knowing there is a chance my girl won't be here - all these people are just obstacles keeping me from leaving to go find her.

"Here, you look like you need this," Jace stumbles up, handing me a red solo cup. Being the son of the undersheriff has made him a little less cautious than the rest of us when it comes to stupid shit. Like drinking beer in the middle of the lawn while all of our parents are up on the deck just thirty yards away.

"Dude, you can't even wait until they all call it a night before you start drinking? Are you trying to piss your dad off again?" I set the cup down, a beer sounds great right now, but I need to be one hundred percent on my A-game when Lenny gets here. I have to convince her that we can beat the odds, she has to know that we were cut from the same cloth. We were made for each other.

"You signed your life away to Uncle Sam, and are getting on a bus to go put yourself through literal hell for the next few weeks - you can have a damn beer, bro." He bends and picks the cup up, handing it back to me. "This is the last time I'm going to see your sorry ass for awhile-"

"Okay, okay," I throw my hands up in defeat, taking the cup back from him before he goes into a full blown toddler tantrum on me. "I will drink a beer with you. But for the sake of not making this weird, please don't get all emotional on me. I already have so much going on with Lenny, I don't know if I could handle you weirding out about me leaving too."

We head toward the end of the dock, stopping about midway to sit and put our feet into the warm August water. Jace seems to be stumbling a little more than I feel comfortable with, so the idea of taking him where the water is over his head doesn't seem like a good one.

"Lennox is… well, she's just Lennox. I'm sure she'll come around, you two have basically been inseparable since the day her family moved here. Speaking of making things weird though, your sister and Quinn? Are they both off limits?" His words are a little slurred and I try to take what he's saying with a grain of salt. He knows those two are just as off limits as Lennox is in my eyes. Not only would I kill him, but if I wasn't around to get the job done, my older brother Will would drive back from college and do it for me.

I let out a noise that sounds like a growl, "Jace, don't fuck with me. You know damn well those three are out of bounds for you. Stay in your own lane brother."

He waves me off, "Yeah, yeah… you and your sports analogy are coming through loud and clear. Not only are you shagging the hottest girl in town, but you also are cock blocking me with two of the others. It's cool though…"

His words fade before he can finish his sentence. "Hey, maybe it's time for you to head inside and sleep whatever this is off."

He stands up - quicker than I expected his inebriated body to move and heads toward the house after saluting me on the way by. "Okay boss, whatever you say." I watch him slither his way up the lawn until he disappears into the slider door underneath the deck, then I stand and make my way to the bonfire where everyone else is.

Well, almost everyone else.

The pit in my stomach grows larger as it starts to set in that I may not see the only person I've ever truly loved, before I step on that bus tomorrow. And as I sit and listen to the people who have been in my life for as long as I can remember talk about college classes, dorm rooms, and roommates, I realize the next few years of my life are going to be dramatically different than theirs. And suddenly it hits me; it's completely unfair to expect Lenny to give up everything she wants, just to be constantly uprooted and moved around the world at the drop of a hat.

As I sit here, staring aimlessly into the oranges and yellows of the fire, I make a silent promise - if Lennox Coleman doesn't come to me before tomorrow morning, I will let her go.

No matter how bad it hurts, I will let her go because that's what you do right? If you love something you set it free with the hope that someday it'll come back to you.

Chapter 1

Lennox

12 years later...

Twelve years.

It's been twelve years since I've stepped foot back in Iron City, Michigan. Even though everything still looks the same, it all feels different. I may have only lived in this small town for less than four years, but for the longest time it was the only place that truly felt like home. This was the place where I met friends that I thought would be in my life forever, I was the captain of the soccer team and class president my senior year. It was where I learned to drive, spent summers out on the lake, but mostly, it was where I fell in love for the first time.

Okay, so the only time.

Here I am knocking on thirty's door in a few short weeks and yes, I shamefully can admit that I've only been in love with one boy. Not to say I haven't tried to love others, but none of them seem to have had that spark I am always searching for. The spark that can light your whole body on fire with just a look or a simple touch.

I know this exists because I've felt it.

It may seem like an entire lifetime ago, but once upon a time, my life seemed perfect. And even if it wasn't perfect, I wouldn't have known because in my eyes any time spent with Graham Thomas was nothing short of magical.

I've spent twelve damn years trying to forget about him, and yet here I am, back in Iron City, sitting in the salon his sister owns, pretending that I'm not still in love with the guy I walked away from all those years ago.

"You ready hot stuff?" Halee lifts the dryer hood. "You're ready to be shampooed out."

"Yep." I stuff my phone back into my purse and follow her towards the shampoo bowls. Looking around this beautiful space she and Quinn have created makes my heart swell with happiness.

Those two were basically inseparable back when we were younger, if they weren't sneaking off to be with Brett and JR, they were trying to tag along with Graham and me.

♡♡♡

"How's the baby? My mom said you had a girl, right?" I've been here for almost two hours and we have been so busy chatting about my life and how devastatingly crappy it is, I haven't even asked her about the child she just gave birth to.

"She's amazing." Her face lights up like any other proud mamas would. "I mean, I may be a little biased, but I'm pretty sure Lauren is perfect. So far she still has my blue eyes but it looks like she may have Luke's dark features. But who knows? She's only a few weeks old so the books say it could all change still."

"I can't wait to meet her." The doorbell dings behind me and I swear Halee's eyes have red hearts coming out of them.

"Well, lucky for you, you don't have to wait very long. Hey sweet pea, come see mommy."

She walks around the desk and past me in what feels like slow motion. Before I can even turn around, I can feel him. His presence. I could always feel him enter a room before I saw or heard him.

As I turn around, our eyes meet and I'm instantly taken back to all those years ago. He looks nothing like the boy I gave my heart to in high school. His hair is longer than I've ever seen it, laying just above his shoulders. His massive, tall, tan, toned body dominates the small waiting area we are standing in, and his eyes… they look like the eyes I used to stare into. But now they seem a little more hollow on the inside than they used to be. Like they've witnessed things that no man or woman should ever have to see in their lifetime. I don't know exactly what he did during his time in the military, but I know one thing, something about Graham Thomas is different.

The last time I saw him was the morning before he left for basic training, the day that changed my life in more ways than one. That day is the reason I've never stepped foot back in this town until now or opened my heart back up to trust another man.

August 17th.

The day that broke me.

Chapter 2

Graham

I've had a shit day. And I mean it literally. A shit day.

When Halee texted first thing this morning asking if I could watch Lauren because Luke had a last minute meeting with his record label, I jumped at the idea of getting some one-on-one time with my angel of a niece. But whatever is coming out of her butt, is rotten. And lucky for me, it decided to also make its way out of her diaper and up her back. Soiling the first two outfits of the day.

As I walk into the door of Studio 365, I feel slightly relieved that I made it through the entire afternoon with my sanity intact and kept this small child alive. I have been on more missions, and seen enough in the last ten years to fill up ten people's lifetimes. Most people who served alongside me would say I'm highly trained and work well under pressure. But something about this small human, who solely depends on me feeding her, changing her, and keeping her safe, it's a bit outside my comfort zone.

When Halee spots us walking in she rushes from around the corner to take Lauren's car seat from me.

I notice *her* almost instantly. Even though Lennox is still facing the opposite direction, I would recognize her from a mile away. She's the same person I've spent nights, more than I'm willing to admit, dreaming about.

When she turns our eyes meet, and they still give everything away just like they used to. They roam up and down my body, drinking every bit of me in, the same way they did the day we met in gym class.

She looks perfect.

From her wavy almond colored hair that now has a few honey colored ends, all the way down to her toes, which are polished in her signature fire engine red she always loved.

The past hits me like a train, and the urge to make her smile takes over. "Hey, sweet lips."

"H-hey, Graham."

I can't look away, no matter how hard I try. There have been so many times in the past twelve years I've wanted to call her, just to see how she was doing. Or when I would visit New York, every part of me wished we would run into each other at a coffee shop and spend the afternoon getting caught up on everything we missed. But now, standing in front of her, I can't seem to think of a single word to say.

I'm not sure how much time has passed when Halee interrupts, "So I take it neither of you knew that the other was in town again?"

"No." "Nope." We both reply, neither willing to look away.

"Well maybe instead of just standing in my lobby, gawking at each other, you could go to Stubs and have a drink. Get caught up on life." Lenny's mouth moves slightly, forming the adorable smirk I remember so well, bringing life to the dimple that takes up her right cheek. "Or maybe you two can just continue to stand here and silently remove each others clothes with your eyes. Whatever works best. Thanks for keeping Lauren for me, Graham. You are a lifesaver."

Halee kisses my cheek, and heads in the direction of the break room with Lauren. "It was great catching up Lenny. I'm so sorry to hear about your dad, let me know if you need anything while you're in town. I'm sure I'll be seeing you around." She turns and winks at me before disappearing around the corner.

I look back at Lennox, but I can't read her like I used to. "What's going on with your dad?"

Her smile fades, "That is a long story."

"Well lucky for you, I have nothing but time today. It's against my better judgment to ever agree with Halee, but maybe we should go grab a drink?" I realize I haven't moved from the doorway after spotting her, when a young woman says "excuse me" and tries to squeeze through.

Lennox glances down at her watch and looks back up to me. "Um… yeah. One drink should be fine. Where do you want to go?"

I open the door and follow her out, "Stubs is just a few blocks away, do you want to walk?"

She lets out a small laugh, "I can't believe that place is still open after all of these years."

We walk into Stubs and I lead her to the back of the bar where we can have a bit of privacy and not have everyone breathing down our necks. I slide into the bench with my back to the wall, old habits die hard. I guess it's just in my blood at this point to sit where I can see everyone in the place, observing all potential exit strategies within seconds.

"Wow." Lennox continues to look around as she sits on the bench across the table from me. "Some things never change, and I guess this bar is one of them."

I can't even begin to focus on what else she is saying because sitting in Iron City, with Lennox Coleman, is too real for me to handle. "You look great Len."

Her cheeks blush and she looks down at the table, picking at some invisible spot in front of her. "Thanks, you look great too."

"How long has it been? Twelve years?"

When her eyes find mine, I see a hint of sadness seeping through her tough exterior she's always worn. "Almost. Crazy, huh?"

"Have you been back at all since you left?" I know I've avoided this town at all costs over the past few years, knowing if I let the idea of the life I could've had back in, I would drown in regrets.

"Nope, up until seven days ago, I left and never looked back. How about you? Do you visit your family often?"

Something is off about her, the light that used to shine from within seems a lot dimmer than it was the last time I saw her. "I come when it's necessary, but never stay longer than a couple of days. This town reminds me of too much, it reminds me of you." The honesty of my own words surprise me.

She swallows and I can see her breathing start to accelerate. I want to ask her why she never came that night, why she ignored my calls and messages the next morning, and why she told her parents not to let me in when I showed up at her house thirty minutes before I needed to get on that damn bus. All I needed was to see her, tell her that our love was strong enough to make this work, and for her to say the same. But I worry if I ask her any of that right now she will get up and walk away, and that will hurt more than it did all those years ago.

Seeing her and talking to her has brought a sense of peace back to me that has been missing for so long. I don't want to do anything to risk losing her again, so I'll stick to a safe topic. "So if you don't mind me poking my nose into your business, why now? What brought you back after all these years of being gone?"

Chapter 3

Lennox

If someone had told me a week ago that I would be back in my hometown, getting my hair done by the girl I always thought would be family someday, and then sitting in Stubs having a drink with Graham Thomas, I would have laughed in their face. But nope, here I am, staring at the man who stars in most of my dreams at night, waiting for something to wake me up.

He is perfect. He always has been, from the minute I laid eyes on him, my first day at Iron City High School. But now he's the grown version of that boy, a chiseled god. Graham has to know I keep checking him out but even the reality of that doesn't stop me. His hair is still sandy blonde but longer, barely brushing his shoulders, his eyes still bright blue like the sky, with little hues of dark blue dancing around the edges. But that's where the familiarity ends. He has always been tall, but as we walked here I noticed he now towers over me. The edges of his shirt are snug around his muscular biceps and although I can't see his abdomen, I'm sure it's just as impressive as the rest of him.

Graham clears his throat, "You just going to keep gawking at me for the remainder of our time or are you going to answer my question?"

I laugh and roll my eyes, "First of all, I'm not gawking. Just taking it all in. You look so much like the same person but so different, it's crazy."

The corner of his mouth lifts, revealing his perfectly white, straight teeth. "And second?"

"Second what?"

"You said first of all, typically that means there's something that follows."

"Oh and second… what was your question?"

The waitress walks over, breaking up the flirtatious banter that seems to come naturally between us. "Sorry about the wait guys, I didn't see you two sneak into this booth. What can I grab ya?"

"I will just take a water please."

Graham looks over at me, "Just a water? You don't want anything stronger for this trip down memory lane?"

"I'm not really much of a drinker." What I really mean is that I haven't had a single drop of alcohol since before the last time I saw him. When people drink they make stupid choices, choices that tend to leave a lifetime of scars on others' lives.

"Oh, okay. Well you know what, how about two waters then." He smiles at the waitress who I'm sure is super annoyed at the fact that we are sitting in a bar, drinking water. "And maybe a bowl of lemons."

After she walks away I say, "You remember?"

"Of course I remember Lenny. There are few things about you that I've forgotten, and you loving two slices of lemon in your water isn't one of them. Now back to our conversation, before you were checking me out - "

"I was NOT checking you out!" I shout, a little louder than I intended to. After I glance over my shoulder, making sure no one is staring, I continue. "It's just great to see you again, that's all. And I believe you asked me why I'm home after all these years, right?"

He chuckles, causing his toned body to shake. "So you were listening."

"I can effectively gawk and listen at the same time." I wink. "Why am I home? Well that's a loaded question. I'm here because my dad was diagnosed a few years ago with early onset Alzheimer's, and up until now, my mom has had a handle on everything. But over the past few months he has really gotten worse, and while Mom would never ask me to come here, I could tell she needed help. So here I am."

"God, Lenny, that's terrible. I'm so sorry. Where's your sister?"

"Oh you know Stacey, she's living her best life out in Colorado. She works for a resort out there, gives ski lessons, and whatever else they need her to do. Every other time I talk to her she has a new flavor of the month, like I said, living her best life. I'm sure she would have walked away from it all, if one of us would've asked. But honestly, she is twenty-three and I don't want her to have to deal with all of this."

The way his eyes dig into me feels like he can see right into my soul. "What about you Len? What did you walk away from? Did all of your dreams come true?"

No.

I want to stand on this table in the middle of this bar and shout to anyone listening. that walking away from Graham Thomas was the biggest mistake of my life. If I would have just come to the party when it started, instead of being such a hard headed brat, the events of that night would have been dramatically different. "Well me, I walked away from a very prestigious law firm in downtown Manhattan, where I just recently became a junior partner. I guess I haven't fully walked away yet, they told me to take some vacation time, and come home. Before this, I never really took days off so I have a lot of vacation stored up. I'm not sure how long their offer will stand, but I am at least here for the next four months. After that, I will re-evaluate and see what I want to do next. I can't imagine leaving, knowing that soon Dad might not even recognize me."

I look up from the spot on the table that I've been staring at, clear my throat and blink away the tears that threaten to overflow. "But enough about me. What about you?"

Just as he starts to talk, he stops, reaching into the side pocket of his cargo shorts to pull out his phone. "I'm sorry, but I have to answer this."

I nod and grab for the water the waitress at some point brought over to the table. Reaching into the bowl, I pull out two lemons and squeeze them into the glass, doing my best to not eavesdrop on Grahams phone call.

"Hey you. I'm good, just catching up with an old friend at Stubs." His words break me in half when I know they shouldn't, am I really just an old friend to him? "That's great babe. I'm glad you are having a good time." Babe? Jesus, he's talking to a woman. Probably his girlfriend or even worse, wife. Of course he is with someone, why wouldn't he be? Obviously he isn't still in love with his high school sweetheart, that would just be pathetic. "I love you too. I'll call you tonight before I go to bed."

He hangs up and sets his phone down on the table. "Sorry about that."

"I should go."

"Wait! Go? Why?"

He places his hand on top of mine as I start to stand up. "This is a bad idea Graham. You obviously have a wife, and I'm sure she wouldn't be at all comfortable with this if you were to elaborate more on who you were with."

He removes his hand from mine, lets out a long sigh and mumbles something under his breath that I can't make out.

"Huh?"

"Not wife… yet. Emma is my fiancè."

Chapter 4

Graham

Is it bad that for the past hour or so, from the moment I set eyes on Lennox, I haven't once thought about Emma?

Sweet Emma. If you looked up "southern belle" in the dictionary I swear her face would be next to it. She doesn't have a hateful bone in her body, she devotes all of her time to her kindergarteners and even when she has a break from that, you will find her at a children's hospital volunteering. When Emma wants to offend someone, she replies with a "bless your heart" or "aren't you sweet", where I'm more likely to just tell someone to fuck off.

And what she's doing with me is a question I have asked myself for the past two years. I don't deserve her, and for the first time in a long while, I wanted to deserve someone. After Lennox walked away - or I left - however you want to place the blame, I spent most of my nights alone or indulging in random hookups with women I hoped I'd never see again. It was easier that way. But when I ran into eyes that basically matched mine, long blonde hair with just enough wave in it to look effortless, I knew something was different about her. She lit a match in my chest that had been burnt out for far too long, and made me excited for the possibility of a future again.

"Fiancé." I look across the table into the heartbroken eyes staring back at me.

"Yeah."

"Sorry, I just… I just thought that by the way you were looking at me and flirting with me, maybe you were still single. I should've known you had someone. I'm sorry, I really should be going. It was great catching up, maybe I'll see you around?"

"Lenny - " I don't want her to leave. Emma sparked my lifeless soul, but seeing Lennox again after all these years just sent a wrecking ball through my chest. "I'm sorry if - " I struggle to find my next words because I know what she's saying is true, I was flirting and I'm sure I was looking at her like I want her.

Part of me does want her. A large part.

The part of me that I tucked deep inside a long time ago. "Please, I want us to do this again. I've missed you. Yes I'm engaged, but that doesn't mean we can't be friends, right?"

She laughs, fucking laughs. "Friends? Do you remember how well that worked out the first time for us?

"Hey Lennox. Thanks for coming to my game."

"You're welcome. I love coming, you know that. I mean, who wouldn't love watching all these guys parade around in tight baseball pants." She elbows me in the rib cage as I wrap my arm around her shoulders.

She has been in Iron City for about five months now and we've spent time together nearly everyday. We kind of agreed on her first day that we would be friends, but I feel like it's so much more than that. I've stopped hanging out with the other girls, and most of our nights consist of me, her, Jace and whatever girl he brings over with him. It looks like we are dating to the outside world, but nothing more than flirty touches happen between us.

"What do you think about coming over tonight? My mom and dad are out of town, and Halee is staying at Quinn's. Other than Will, we will have the house to ourselves." I raise my eyebrows at her, hoping she catches onto the fact I would love to spend some more one on one time with her.

"Sounds good. Is Jace coming too?" She climbs up into the passenger side of my truck. My parents thought it would be best if I waited a year before starting kindergarten so I have my license before the majority of my classmates.

"I didn't invite him. I was kind of hoping maybe we could just chill and watch a movie. Just the two of us?" I start up the truck, avoiding looking in her direction. This is the first time either of us has suggested anything that would result into moving past the friend zone. But believe me, I've wanted to.

"Oh. Okay. That's cool with me. I'll call my parents when we get to your house and let them know. Can you take me home after the movie?"

I glance over at her and smile. "I would love to."

"Cool."

When I walk from the bathroom to my bedroom I glance down the hall to see if I can see Lennox in the kitchen. When we got here, I told her to make herself at home while I jumped in the shower to clean off the sweat and grime from the game. But as I walk through my bedroom door, I see her laying on my bed looking at the Sports Illustrated magazine that was on my nightstand.

"Whatcha lookin' at?" When she sees me with nothing but a towel wrapped around my waist her adorable cheeks pink and she quickly looks away.

"Oh God. Sorry Graham. I should've waited in the living room, but your brother got home and it was just kind of awkward with him and his girlfriend out there making out on the couch next to me - "

I walk over and sit down on the bed next to her, "Stop. Don't be sorry. You can just turn your head while I put on some shorts. Unless you want me to stick to just the towel?"

She swats my bare chest and smiles. "Put some clothes on loser, I will turn away."

"Okay, okay but no peeking Coleman, I would hate for you to see something you like and want more." What I really mean, is please look, and see exactly everything you want and never want it from anyone else.

"Psst. Please. Like I would even know what I'm looking for in that department."

She has her back to me as she flips through the rest of the magazine she had when I walked in, and I plop down on the bed next to her in nothing but my basketball shorts. "What do you mean, you don't know what you're looking for?"

Her cheeks blush for the second time, and she turns away from me. I pull her arm lightly so she falls into my lap. "Really Len. What do you mean?"

"God Graham, are you seriously going to make me say it?" I lift my eyebrows encouragingly. "Okay fine, I've never seen a penis before. There, are you happy?"

"You're a virgin?" I kind of suspected but the topic has never been brought up in conversation.

"Yeah, why is that so hard to believe? Not everyone loses their V-card the summer going into high school. Some of us want to wait until it's with someone special, maybe so it actually means something."

With her head still in my lap, I brush away the pieces of hair that have fallen in her face. "Oh yeah, tell me, am I someone special to you? Because you're pretty damn special to me." I trace my thumb around the edge of her lips, silently begging for her to say yes.

"I - " Her tongue darts out to wet her lips and briefly makes contact with my thumb. "I thought we were just friends?"

She sits up and I notice the way her chest is rising and falling quicker than it was before. I place the palm of my hand on the side of her cheek and slowly pull her head closer to me. "I don't just want to be your friend anymore Lenny. In fact, I'm pretty sure I never wanted to JUST be friends. I want to kiss you, and hold your hand in public, I want everyone to know that I'm yours and you're mine. Please tell me you feel the same way."

I lean my head in the rest of the way so our foreheads are touching but nothing else. I so badly want her to open her eyes and look at me, maybe then I would know what she was thinking, but instead she keeps them closed and focuses on her breathing. "I want that too." She finally whispers.

A smile so big it hurts takes over my face. "I'm sorry, I didn't hear that. Could you maybe say it again, only louder this time?"

Her rich brown eyes open, and tell me everything I need to know. She wants this just as badly as I do. "I want to be more than friends, too. But you have to realize, I'm nowhere near as experienced as you when it comes to all of this. And even though we are what... dating? Doesn't mean I want to jump right into bed with you."

"Uh... Len, you're already in my bed."

She goes to lean back, but I pull her down so we are both laying and lean up on one elbow to look at her face to face. "We can go as slow or as fast as you want us to."

Her voice is shaky, "You're okay with that?"

"One hundred percent okay with that."

"Okay, but I think… I think I'd really like you to kiss me now, if that's okay?"

I laugh and lean in, kissing the tip of her nose on the way down. "Perfect, because I would really like to kiss you now."

And when our lips meet, it's unlike any other kiss I've had. She's shy at first, timid almost, as our lips gently get to know each other for the first time. But as I slowly slip my tongue in to meet hers, something changes in her. Without ever removing her lips from mine, she pushes me so my back is against the bed and climbs on top of me, her legs straddling my waist.

My hands work their way from her back, down to her round ass and back up. Just when she takes things further than I expected and starts to grind her hips into my now growing erection, my bedroom door swings open.

"Whoa! I heard noises in here but I half expected it to be Graham and Jace, not the two of you." Will says slyly while leaning up against the door frame.

Lennox jumps off and I grab a pillow to cover the fully present boner in my shorts. "Dude, ever heard of knocking?"

"Yeah, but what's the fun in that? You two want pizza? Mom and Dad left money for us to order in, or are you guys going to skip dinner and dry hump in here all night?" Will's girlfriend comes around the corner to join the party.

"Pizza sounds great, but can you two get the hell out? We will meet you in the kitchen in a few minutes."

Will laughs as he shuts the door, "At least use a condom baby brother, Mom and Dad will kill you if you knock someone up in high school."

I fall back onto the bed and let my arm fall over my face. Lennox curls up into my side, draping her leg over mine. "Sorry about that. He's such a dick sometimes."

She giggles, a sound that I could listen to for the rest of my life. "It's okay. We probably needed that cool down anyways, with how quickly things were moving and all. But that was fun, we should definitely do it more."

I flip her around so this time I'm the one straddling her, pinning her arms with my hands and pepper her neck with kisses. "Oh you better believe we will be doing that all the time, sweet lips."

"Sweet lips?"

"Yeah, I'm not sure what chapstick you have on, but your lips taste like candy."

"Hmm... well if you are going to call me sweet lips, I think it's only fair that I get to pick out a nickname for you." She taps her chin with her index finger while purposely trying to look deep in thought. "I got it... Graham cracker!"

"That's a terrible nickname." I lean in and kiss her, suddenly not able to keep my mouth away from hers.

"Don't care. I'm sticking with it."

"Len, as long as you stick with me, you can call me whatever you want. You make me feel things I've never felt before."

"Don't worry, Graham cracker, I'm not going anywhere."

"Yeah, sweet lips. I remember the last time we tried to be just friends." Judging by the look on her face, she was just reliving the same memory I was. "But the difference is, this time, we aren't just two horny teenagers. I promise, I can keep this relationship platonic if you can. Because you have to know, I can't imagine not having you in my life again. Especially when we are going to be living just miles from each other for at least the next few months."

She puts her hand out to shake mine, "Friends. I kinda like the sound of that Graham cracker."

Yeah. She was definitely just thinking about the first time we kissed. As much as I want to keep Lennox Coleman in my life, I think being just friends with her now, is going to be just as difficult as it was the first time. But now, there's another heart involved, and that's one heart I refuse to hurt just because the one that got away, just walked back into my life.

Chapter 5

Lennox

"I'm so glad you agreed to come out with us tonight. I haven't had a girls' night in so long, and with Luke being off this weekend it was perfect. All the men are at my house, playing daddy daycare and we're going out on the town." Halee was basically bouncing up and down as we walked into Stubs.

I wouldn't necessarily call going to Stubs a *night out on the town*, but after just having a baby a couple months ago, I'm sure she needs whatever time away she can get. "Thanks for basically dragging me out of my parents' house. I've become such a homebody since I got here. When I was in New York, I was always working, but here, it's kinda nice to just lay low and hang around the house. Who's all going to be here tonight?"

We walk past the pool tables and I spot a large group of girls gathered around the corner booth in the back. My mind drifts back to earlier in the week when Graham and I sat in this bar, doing what I briefly thought was rekindling what we once had. Okay, so maybe it was just a hopeful idea, but who am I kidding? Even if Graham wasn't engaged, I'm damaged goods, there is no way he would want anything to do with me if he knew the truth.

"Oh. My. God." One of the women squeals as she jumps up and runs towards me. "Hales told me you were back in town, but I had no idea you were coming tonight." She pulls away, allowing me to get a good look at her face.

"Quinn?"

"Duh. Who else would it be? Come on, come sit down and meet everyone else."

Over the next ten minutes I meet Charlie, whose real name is Charlotte but apparently the only person that gets away with calling her that is JR. And the other woman is Annie, Luke's sister. She isn't nearly as open when it comes to sharing personal information as these other girls seem to be.

Quinn places her elbows on the table and her chin in her hands, looking at me like she's ready to hear the dirt. "So Lennox, have you seen Graham yet?" Her eyebrows bounce up and down.

Halee slaps her best friend in the arm, "Q, come on. She just got here, can you at least give her time to have a couple drinks before you go deep diving into her personal life?"

I laugh, "It's okay Halee, I don't mind. Yes, he and I sat down and chatted earlier this week, after we ran into each other at the salon. I had just gotten my hair done, and he was bringing sweet, little Lauren back to Halee."

All four sets of eyes are on me, "Annnnnd…" Charlie asks.

"And we caught up on... a lot. It was nice."

"Nice?" Quinn looks at me like she's confused. "Just, nice? You saw the first man you ever loved for the first time in over ten years and it was just... nice? Sounds like you're leaving something out."

"Right. You all know Graham is engaged to someone right? So get rid of whatever idea you have playing out in your dirty heads right now about how the two of us got to know each other again. We agreed to be friends."

This time Halee lets out the obnoxious laugh, "Friends? The two of you? That'll be the day.

I don't know how many times I walked in on you two all over each other when we were growing up. Mom and Dad used to scold Graham every other day because of your guys PDA. I'm giving this whole friendship thing a month, tops!"

"What part of engaged did you guys miss? Off the market. Not available. Besides, I don't even know how long I'll be in town for."

Quinn shrugs her shoulders, "He's not off the market yet, and from what Hales said, she isn't what he needs."

What does that mean? I want to ask but I know if I allow myself to go down this rabbit hole I won't be able to find my way back out. The fact of the matter is, Graham is engaged to Emma, and he and I agreed to be friends.

End of story.

Maybe if I keep telling myself that, one of these days I'll start to actually believe it.

"I have a fun idea, I saw this question on one of the Facebook groups I'm in today. If you came with a warning label, what would it be?" Thank God for Charlie and her ability to move the conversation in a different direction.

"Ohhhh… this is fun. I'll go first." Quinn pauses while she tries to think of what her warning label would be. "Mine would probably be 'Warning: frequent adult language' or 'Warning: may contain alcohol.'"

We all laugh, and Annie jumps in next, "My warning label would for sure be, 'Warning: doesn't think before speaking.'"

"That is definitely you," Halee chimes. "Mine is, 'Warning: tread lightly, she could blow at any moment."

They all turn and look at me, "Um… I'm not sure."

Quinn grunts, "Oh, come on Lenny, just say whatever comes to your mind first."

"Warning: doesn't share well with others." As I say the words, I instantly regret them. Graham isn't mine to share anymore, but I know that's exactly what I meant when I said it.

♡♡♡

We make our way up the cobblestone walkway toward Halee's house. Good thing I'm not much of a drinker because these girls were a hot mess tonight. Annie cut herself off after about three, but the other girls kept taking shot after shot like we were all still in college. I hope they enjoyed tonight because I have a feeling they will deeply regret their actions in the morning.

"You know what I think?" The words stumble out of Halee's drunken lips. Before I have a chance to answer, she continues, "I don't think Graham is really in love with Emma, I think he has just settled with her because he thought he could never have you again."

I laugh, "Well you know what I think? I think you are really drunk, and you probably don't mean the words that are coming out of your mouth right now. He seems happy, and that's all I've ever wanted for him."

"Happy?! Really? If you wanted him to be happy then why did you walk away all those years ago Lennox? He loved you, shit, he still loves you. I can see it clear as day when he looks at you."

We finally make it to the top step of her front porch, "Come on, let's get you inside so you can sleep this off."

Halee yanks her arm out of mine and turns, pulling me so I am looking directly at her. She might be a tiny little thing but she definitely has some strength behind her, maybe it's just the adrenaline from the alcohol. "I'm not going inside until you tell me the reason you never showed up that night. You know he sat there, at that damn bonfire for hours, just staring at the hill, hoping you would be the one walking down it. But you never came. Why? Were you that selfish that you couldn't even bring yourself to come say goodbye?"

"Halee, I can't talk about this right now. There are things that you don't know and - "

The front door opens and there stands Graham, in dark denim jeans, a white T-shirt, and barefoot with perfectly tousled hair. "Hey guys. What's going on? It sounded like someone was shouting out here."

I lightly nudge Halee through the door, "Nothing, I just drove her home since I didn't drink and she might have had a little more than she planned on." By now, our little drunk companion has disappeared down the hallway, leaving the two of us standing awkwardly by the front door. "Alright, well I suppose I'm going to walk back to my parents. See ya later Graham."

"Wait!"

I turn back around.

"Give me a couple minutes to make sure Luke is all set and I can drive you home. You don't need to be walking right now, it's after midnight."

I let out a giggle, "Really? How many times have I made this walk, I'm sure I will be just fine. Plus if someone comes up in a creepy van, I won't take the bait if they offer me candy. But if they say anything about tacos, all bets are off."

"Seriously, Lenny. Please just let me drive you home. I'm leaving anyway, and it would make me feel better knowing you got there safely. Please."

I throw my arms up in surrender, "Alright, alright, I will go get in the truck. Take your time."

I decide against getting in the truck and drop the tailgate, crawling into the bed. The clear sky and stars are definitely something I never thought I would miss when I moved to New York, but I do. Graham's voice startles me as I search for the Little Dipper, "Whatcha doin' back there sweet lips?"

I turn my head to find him leaning along the side, "Admiring the stars. There isn't much stargazing done back in the city."

"Come on, jump out. I have an idea."

He holds his hand out to me as I jump down off the tailgate, "Do you trust me Lennox?"

I laugh, "Well that seems like a loaded question. Should I trust you?"

"Get in the truck Coleman."

"I can't believe you still have this old thing."

He smiles but his eyes never leave the road, "This is a 1980 Chevy Silverado, why wouldn't I still have her? She's a beauty. Plus, I've had a lot of great memories inside this cab and in the bed of this truck."

My heart flutters, as I remember the first time he made love to me.

"Graham, where the heck are we going? And why am I blindfolded?"

"Patience sweet lips. We're almost there."

I can tell we are walking on grass, but I have no idea what this crazy guy of mine is up to. When he called earlier and asked if I wanted to come over, I assumed we would be doing our usual, watching movies and snacking on everything in the fridge. But this time when I pulled into his driveway he was standing there, with a single red rose, and a blindfold.

"Alright, here we are."

Once my eyes adjust, I find his truck backed down to the lake, with pillows and blankets covering the inside of the bed. "What's all this?"

"Well my parents are out and won't be back until late, Halee is gone for the night, so it's just us. I thought maybe we could watch the sunset back here."

I turn and wrap my arms around his neck, pulling him down so our noses are touching, "Oh yeah, that's what you thought we might do down here?" His strong arms pull me in, and his lips find mine. In the two years I've known Graham his body has already gone through so many changes. Not only has he sprouted up, now hitting close to six-foot-two, but thanks to all the sport training he does, even his muscles have muscles.

"You know there is never any pressure with me and you Lenny. But the last couple times we've gotten really close, so with the chance that tonight could be the night, I wanted it to be special. And if we crawl up into the bed of the truck and nothing happens other than we watch the sunset and eat all the crap I took out of the cabinet, that's cool with me too. I'm just excited for some alone time. Lately Jace seems to always be around."

"I think it's all perfect. Thank you." I turn and pull his hand, tugging his large frame in the direction of the tailgate. He effortlessly lifts me up and I crawl to the top where there is easily over a dozen pillows stacked up. "Where did all of these come from?"

"Inside," he laughs, "We should probably put them back before my parents get home or my mom will have my ass. Do you want anything to eat?"

"No, I think I'm okay right now." I curl my body into the side of his, adjusting slightly, trying to find the perfect place to lay my head. My stomach is doing flips at the idea of tonight being the night. Graham has been so patient with me, for so long, knowing that taking the next step was a big deal, he hasn't once pushed me. I know he's the person I want to lose my virginity to, I just need to get out of my own head and let things happen naturally tonight.

"What's going on in that pretty head of yours?"

"Oh, I don't know, just everything. I'm scared and nervous, but excited at the same time."

He brushed a few pieces of hair out of my face, "What about this has you scared? Maybe I can ease your mind a little."

"What if it hurts?" I can feel my cheeks redden. I may not be overly experienced in this department, but I listen when my friends talk about their first time, some of them even bled a little. The idea of bleeding seems so much more embarrassing than anything else.

"I'm not going to lie and say that it won't hurt, because I have no idea. But I promise you, if it does, we will stop or go slower, whatever you want. I would never want to hurt you Lenny, ever."

I sit up, yanking my shirt up and over my head, and pull my denim shorts down around my ankles. Leaving me sitting in front of Graham in just my lacy bra and underwear. Since the last time things got close to the next level, I have made it a point to be on my A game when it comes to my undergarments.

His eyes widen and he grabs a blanket, covering me up, "Jesus, Len. It's not completely dark out yet. What if my pervy neighbor just saw you?"

I laugh and pull him back down so we are laying again, "Will you touch me?"

I don't have to say much more, he quickly sheds his clothes, throwing them in a pile next to mine at the end of the truck. He lifts the corner of the blanket and slides underneath, only wearing his boxers. When our skin touches, my whole body feels like it bursts into flames, and the anticipation of what comes next hits me all at once.

We lay here, gazing at the setting sun that's quickly disappearing behind the tree line across the lake for what seems like forever. He seems to be perfectly content with the intimate closeness we are sharing, but shockingly I'm not. It's like a switch inside of me has flipped and the need of wanting more consumes me. I want him, all of him, and I want it now.

I slide my once timid hand under the blanket and slowly work it down his defined chest. I reach his boxer line, which is typically where I would stop, but not tonight. No, tonight I won't let my fear of the unknown stop me. I gently lift the edge and lower my hand underneath to find his already growing erection.

It's larger than I expect. Over the last couple years I've felt it through his clothes, and although his hands have wandered below my waistline a couple times, this is the farthest I have ever ventured.

"Lenny, are you sure about this?" His voice for the first time seems shaky and unsure. "I don't want you to think-"

I latch my lips to his, stopping his words before they can leave his mouth. I don't want to think about any of it, because if I do; if I think about the fact that we could be caught at any moment by someone in his family, the logical side of me might force us to stop. And the butterflies in my stomach and the pulse I feel between my legs are a sure sign that I don't want this to stop.

"Don't talk Graham, don't even think. Just do... do whatever you want to do to me. Please. I'm so ready for this."

Apparently that's all he needed to hear because within seconds he flips us so I'm on my back and he's hovering above me. His hand slides behind my back, unclasping my bra with one hand, which he then tosses over the side of the truck. That should be fun to find in the dark later.

His hands cup my now bare breasts, gently massaging and pulling on my nipples. "You're perfect, Lennox Coleman. I love you so much"

No matter how many times he has said it, I will never tire of hearing it. Some might say that at seventeen we are too young to really know what love is, and that may be true. But whatever this is, whatever I feel with this boy, I never want to feel anything else, with anyone else. Graham Thomas is my forever. "I love you, too."

He sits back on his heels as he slowly removes my underwear, thankfully tossing them to the side, not throwing them into the yard with my bra. "I have to get you wet sugar lips. It won't hurt as bad if you are wet, but remember, if at anytime you want to stop, just say the word."

His fingers lightly slide over my mound, parting me, spreading the wetness that has already taken up residency. "You are so wet already Len."

"Please, don't stop." My back arches as he slides one finger, and then two inside of me. I open my legs wider, granting him all the access he needs to continue. His lips fall onto one of my tight nippes, and work their way to the other. "Oh, God, Graham." My stomach starts to tighten and my legs begin to tremble.

"That's right, babe. Just let go." His thumb grazes over my clit, sending me over the edge. My entire body trembles and suddenly I feel like the entire surface of my skin in on fire, in the best possible way.

When I finally start to come down, he places his lips to mine. "How was that?"

"Amazing." I try to catch my breath. "Why haven't we done that sooner?"

He sits up, removes his boxers and reaches into his pants pocket to retrieve a silver packet. Waving it in the air, he says, "Condom. Can't be too careful, ya know." He winks, before his face gets serious. "But if we are going to do this as often as I'd like to, you may want to think about getting on birth control too. Just to be safe."

I smile, "Got it."

I watch him closely as he rips open the foil and rolls the condom down his shaft. Now I know this may be the first time I've ever seen a penis, other than in a health book, but his seems large. Panic sets in as he maneuvers his body over mine, parting my legs with his, the tip of his erection nudging where his fingers just were. "Are you okay?"

I take a deep breath, "Yeah, just nervous. But I want this, I promise I want this. Just go slow."

He places his forehead to mine and I start to feel a pressure build inside of me as he enters. "Still okay?"

I take a deep breath, and exhale slowly. "Yes, just keep going slow."

"I'm about halfway in."

Good Lord, only halfway.

He continues to carefully guide the rest of himself in, "There, I'm in. How do you feel?"

"Full, so full. But it feels good."

Graham's hips start to move, forming a rhythm that makes my head spin. It hurts so good, is the best way to describe it. Like we are fully connected, not knowing where he starts and where I end. "Damn Lenny, you are so tight. I'm not going to last long."

The friction of his skin rubbing my already sensitive clit, plus the fullness of him being inside of me is overwhelming enough, but when his fingers pinch my taunt nipple it sends me over the orgasmic cliff again. My toes point, causing my legs to straighten, and my insides do backflips, repeating the same sensation as before only this time stronger.

As my body relaxes, I feel him twitch inside of me. "Did you - ?"

His breathing is rapid, and he struggles to get it back under control. "That, sweet lips - " he places a tender kiss on my forehead, and slides out of me, discarding the condom. " - was amazing. It's never felt that... intense before. I was pretty sure my heart was going to stop there at the end."

He doesn't give me time to over analyze what just happened, instead he slips back underneath the blanket and pulls me into his side. "Thank you."

"For what?" He turns his body slightly so we are facing each other.

"For being you, for waiting until I was ready, for tonight, and every other night after this. Thank you for being you, Graham cracker. I love you so much."

And I did. In the depths of my soul, I knew there would never be another person who could compare to this guy right here.

He's my everything.

"No, thank you. Thank you for being someone worth waiting for, thank you for making this easy. You make everything easy Len, *the days, the nights, they all seem so much more simple since the day you walked into that gym class. I love you, too"*

The change in texture underneath the tires wakes me out of my dream. Did I fall asleep? That's a night I've replayed so many times over the years, but just now seemed so vivid, like I was really there, reliving that moment with him.

"Where are we?" I ask as he pulls down a dirt road.

"Taking a detour, I thought maybe we could look at the stars."

"I really should be getting home Graham, it's close to one in the morning."

He laughs, parks the truck, turning off the headlights. "Oh come on Len, what's the worst that could happen, you might get grounded? Just tell your parents you were with me, they always had a soft spot in their hearts when it came to me."

A smile tugs at the corners of my mouth because I know he's right. Graham could do no wrong in Mom and Dad's eyes, never could. Anytime we were having a disagreement in high school they would say "What did you do this time Lennox".

God forbid it was his fault.

"Are we at the baseball practice fields?"

"Yep, best place to look at the stars."

"Can't we get in trouble for being out here?"

After letting out a boisterous laugh, Graham jumps out of the truck, "Come on sugar lips, where's your sense of adventure?" Reaching behind the seat, he pulls out a blanket and shuts the door.

I sit there for a few seconds, contemplating my next move. I know I could ask him to get back in the truck and take me home, and he would. But is that really what I want?

Everything inside of me screams no.

My door opens, "Huh?" Graham is holding one of his large hands out to me.

"Huh, what?"

"Where's your sense of adventure these days, Lenny?"

I take his hand, feeling the fireworks that are silently exploding inside of me when our skin touches, "For this kind of thing? Um… I probably left it somewhere back in high school."

I hear a light chuckle as he helps me up onto the lowered tailgate.

After he joins me, Graham spreads the blankets across our laps and then lays back. Him taking in the view of the stars, me taking in the view of him.

He was wrong. The worst that could happen isn't me getting "adult grounded".

No.

My worst case scenario just happened… I just realized I've never stopped loving this man. Not for one second, of one day, in all the years we've been apart. Graham is a part of me, embedded into my soul. And to make things worse, this man I long for is untouchable, because he belongs to another woman, someone who isn't damaged goods.

Chapter 6

Graham

I know this is a terrible idea. Laying this close to Lennox Coleman could possibly be the worst idea I've had in a long time. Everything down to my core is drawn to her, like we are magnets and no matter what happens we'll always find our way back to each other.

But it's too late. Too much time has passed and now I have Emma, my sweet Emma. How would she feel if she knew I was laying in the bed of my truck with Lennox? Laying in the exact spot where we made love for the first time, and many times again after that. I'm wading in deadly water right now, I know it, but that pull continues - and no matter how hard I try to keep my distance - here we are.

"What is your fiancé doing right now?" Obviously her ability to read my mind hasn't faded over the years.

"Well, she is probably sleeping, considering it's also the middle of the night in South Carolina." I look over and smile. Luckily for me, she continues gazing at the night sky. I quickly look back up, knowing if our eyes meet, I will be a goner.

"Can I ask what you are doing up here while she's still down there?"

"Well, to make a long story short, I came back to Michigan a few months sooner so I could find a house, and she wanted to stay until the school year ended."

She turns her head in my direction without moving the rest of her body, but I continue looking forward. "It's almost July, Graham... shouldn't school be over by now?" I let out a sigh, "Sorry, I know this isn't really any of my business."

"No, it's okay. That wasn't directed at you, more like the situation. She was supposed to be up here by June, schools down there get out a lot earlier than the ones up here. But apparently she got offered a summer school position that she couldn't leave behind. She claims this will be the closure she needs to walk away." I place my hands behind my head, trying to keep myself from reaching out and grabbing her hand that just lightly skimmed past mine.

"Does she not want to move up here? I guess I don't understand why she wouldn't want to be wherever you are. Or vice versa."

I laugh, her bluntness is one of the qualities that first drew me to her. "No, I don't think Michigan is exactly her choice of where we should settle down. But she loves me and knows that I need this. After - " Do I really want to go there with her right now? Am I ready to open up about what happened with Dean last year? " - I just needed to be around family and familiar things after the year I had."

"Do you want to talk about it?" She's now shifted on her side, with her head propped up on her hand. *Don't make eye contact Thomas, you will fall in way too deep.* I say the chant over and over again in my head.

"Maybe another time."

"Okay."

She rotates to her back, leaving this situation feeling slightly less intimate. "What about you? How's your dad doing these days?"

"Not great. His memory is slipping more and more everyday, most of the time he doesn't even know who Mom and I are. I think that is probably the hardest thing. The other day he wet his pants," she laughs, but I know her, it's probably just to avoid facing her real emotions head on. "The doctors said that in these late stages, it's common for a person to forget things as basic as when to use the restroom. Eventually I guess his body will just forget how to breathe. Can you imagine? Forgetting how to breathe. It's one of the simplest things in the world that we all take for granted because we don't have to think about it. Our body just knows what to do and it does it. But what happens when your body no longer knows? You die."

I can feel the pain in her words as she speaks them. Her dad has always been her real life hero, she's a daddy's girl through and through. And now she has to watch the man who has lived on a pedestal most of her life, wither away into a shell of the person he used to be.

"We used to laugh," she continues. "I know I wasn't home, but we talked on the phone at least every other day while I was away. He was always so excited to know about Columbia, and then when I started at the law firm he would always ask about my cases even though he said all of that law mumbo jumbo was way above his pay grade. And now, most days, he looks at me like I'm some stranger living in his home. I know losing him will be hard, but we've already lost him. Maybe not in the physical sense, but the man we love is no longer alive."

I hear the slightest sniffle and her hand reaches up to wipe a tear from the corner of her eye. I reach out, catching her hand with mine on it's way back down. Everything inside of me knows this is dangerous, that I shouldn't touch her, but I can't help it. Watching her world break around her, knowing there is nothing I can do about it, doesn't sit well with me.

"Look at me."

She slowly turns her head and her glossy brown eyes meet mine. I want to reach out and somehow wipe the pain away.

"You light up your dads world Lennox." She goes to say something but I stop her, "Just listen for a second. You're the apple of his eye, and even though it doesn't seem like it right now, your dad is still inside there, and he still loves you more than anything else in this world. I know this has to be hard, but just try to focus on the good times, and maybe try and make whatever memories you can before he's gone."

Tears spill over the rims of her eyes and I throw caution to the wind, reaching across to wipe them away. We are only inches away from each other and the pull between us is at an all time high.

Her tongue darts out, wetting her already inviting lips. "Graham - " But before I realize what's happening my mouth is on hers. She opens up to me the same way she did all those years ago, letting out a slight moan as I pull on her bottom lip with my teeth.

Everything about this moment feels right, except it's not. "Shit. Emma." I pull away quickly, jump off the tailgate into the grass where I start pacing. What the hell am I doing? Why do I feel so out of control with my body right now? I know I shouldn't want this, but I do.

"Hey." Lennox stands in front of me, stopping me with her hands on my stomach. When I look down at the contact she quickly pulls her hands away. "It's okay. This is okay. I mean it's not, but it didn't mean anything. We both were feeling vulnerable and had a moment of weakness, it won't happen again."

She's right. It won't happen again, it can't. Emma will be moving up here, leaving the only place she's ever known, to be with me in just a few short weeks. I need to get my head out of my ass and keep my distance from Lenny. She was right, her and I being just friends isn't possible. There is too much history and chemistry between us. The little voice inside my head is screaming "Then why are you marrying another woman?!" but I ignore it. I asked Emma to be my wife, she's stuck by me through one of the hardest years of my life, and she loves me - that's why I'm marrying her.

"But do you love her?" Lennox's voice drags me out of my downward spiral.

"What?"

"You just listed all the reasons why you are marrying her, but not one of them was because you love her?" Damn. Did I just say all of that out loud? "Graham, look at me. Do you love her?"

The answer should be simple. If anyone would've asked me a couple weeks ago if I was in love with my fiancé, the answer would have been yes. Simple and easy. But looking into the rich brown eyes starring back at me, I know nothing about this is simple or easy. I love Emma, but will I ever be capable of loving her the way I have loved

Lennox since we were sixteen-years-old? Is it possible to be in love with two very different women at one time? Without knowing the answer to any of these, I reply to her question the only way I know how.

"Yes."

Chapter 7

Lennox

Last night was rough.

Well the kiss was unlike anything else I've felt in a long time, but everything after that, went downhill quickly. Why would I ask him if he loved Emma? Of course he loves her, he's marrying her.

The ride home was probably the most awkward it's ever been between the two of us. It was obvious he didn't know what to say and I was at a complete loss for words. Never did I imagine coming back to Iron City and seeing Graham again would stir up all these feelings I was positive I let go of eleven years ago. But here I am, feeling just as heartbroken as the day he got on that bus, knowing I would probably never see him again.

I never had any intention of coming back here after that night.

Unfortunately things change, so I find myself lying on an unfamiliar bed, in the same room I used to sleep in while in high school. At least they made a good choice of redecorating after I left, the neon green, orange and black probably wasn't the best choice in colors in hindsight.

My phone vibrates on the nightstand.

Halee Thomas: Hey, hey, hey! My parents are having a cookout today and wanted me to invite you. My mom said no excuses, get your butt over there at three. Don't worry about bringing a dish to pass, you know her, she has enough food to feed an army.

I can't face Graham after how we ended things last night. He pulled into my parents driveway, put the truck in park and said, "Well I guess I'll see you around," without even glancing in my direction. I smiled, wishing I could say everything that was on my mind, but knowing I shouldn't. I made my way up the walkway, onto my parents' front porch and turned back to look at him. He just stayed there, parked, looking forward, lost in a gaze. I heard him back out of the driveway once I was inside.

Does he feel it too? The incessant need to be with one another? How can we spend so long apart and be fine but two weeks back in the same town and we can't seem to keep the distance we both know we need?

But were we ever really fine?

Me: Please tell your mom I said thank you for thinking about me, but it's probably best I keep my distance for awhile. I'm sorry.

Halee Thomas: Distance from Graham?

Me: Yeah.

Halee Thomas: Well my brooding brother won't even be here today. He had some lame excuse on why he couldn't come. Not sure of the details. Come on Len. Mom and dad would love to see you, and it's Luke, Lauren and I, and my brother Will and his family. Quinn said her and Walker might swing over, but it's Sunday and he just got off a long shift, so I doubt they will even get out of bed today. (eye roll emoji)

I wonder what reason Graham has for missing out on his family's cookout. But if he isn't going to be there, I don't see the harm in going. It really would be great to see Ed and Catherine again, those two became like second parents to me all those years ago.

Me: Okay, okay. I surrender. See you at three.

Halee Thomas: Cool. Don't forget your suit. The lake is perfect right now.

The smell of bacon wafts into my room from downstairs, so I decide it's time to peel my lazy butt out of bed and head down. It's just after nine but considering I didn't get home until almost three and then laid in bed reliving that kiss until around five, I'm still feeling exhausted. Nothing a little breakfast can't help, then I will shower and get around for this afternoon.

"Good morning sweetie." My mom says from behind the stove. "I was hoping the smell would bring you down."

I look around the kitchen and then out into the living room, "Where's dad?"

She gives me a sympathetic smile, "He's not having a good morning. Maybe this afternoon will be better."

"The Thomas family invited me over for a cookout, but I don't have to go if you need me here today? I'm sure they will understand."

My mom sets a plate with scrambled eggs, bacon and toast down in front of me and I take a moment to really look at her. The smile lines around her eyes are looking more prominent than when I saw her back at Christmas, and that little crease in her forehead that she always got when she was worried seems to be a permanent feature lately. "Oh no, you should go. When is the last time you saw all of them? I'm sure they miss you. Your father and I will be just fine today. He had a rough night, so I would bet he will sleep most of the afternoon anyways. You won't miss anything exciting around here sweetie."

"You know you don't have to be so strong Mom. It's okay to break a little." I place my hand on top of hers. "That's why I'm here. To help take a little bit off of your plate."

She picks up a piece of bacon, holding it inches from her mouth. "None of this should be put on you or your sister. Plus, I know how much you hate this town after what happened. If it becomes too much to handle, just say the word and we will get you out of here."

"Momma, I'm fine. It helps that he doesn't live here anymore. I don't have to worry about running into him." I try to think of a way to change the topic, knowing I don't like where it's going.

"How was your night with Graham?" Well that wasn't exactly the topic change I was looking for but what the hell.

"How did you - ?"

She puts her hand up to stop me, "I'm your mother, and no matter how old you are, when you are staying in this house, I will wait up for you. I saw him drop you off, and it was well after two." I shrug my shoulders and continue to push my food around the plate with my fork. "That's a hard and bumpy road you are driving down Lennox Louise, and unless you are truly capable of letting him back in and telling him what happened and the real reason you didn't show up that night, I don't think it's fair to either of you to dredge up the past."

"We just went to look at the stars and talk momma." And had a searing hot kiss but she didn't need to know that part. "Plus, he's engaged. Her name is Emma, she's a sweet, southern, kindergarten teacher, and is exactly what he needs. Someone like her. Not me, I'm nothing but damaged goods. Even if I did want something again with him, you and I both know I'm not capable of that anymore."

And then it hits me like a Mac Truck. Last night when we kissed, nothing happened. I didn't start sweating, I didn't have a panic attack, I didn't scream, the world didn't go black - I was fine. I haven't been able to kiss a man without anxiety and flashbacks creeping in since before that night.

"Lenny, I really wish you would stop referring to yourself as damaged goods. And maybe you should rethink about talking to someone again. I know it didn't go well the first time around but it's been years. It might be time."

Here's my mom, carrying the weight of the world on her shoulders with everything going on with my dad and she is still trying to fix me. The problem is, I'm not fixable. But instead of telling her that, I just smile and say, "I will think about it momma."

But I won't. There are only three people in this world who know what happened to me eleven years ago. My mom, the shrink that my mom forced me to talk to that year, and *him*. No one else can know about it or the events that took place three months later, especially not Graham.

He would never forgive me.

Chapter 8

Lennox

As I pull into the driveway of a house that once felt like a second home to me, the butterflies fluttering about in my stomach start to feel like pterodactyls. Knowing Graham is not going to be here, calmed me for a brief second on the drive over, but now part of me feels like I'm stepping over some imaginary line that we have drawn in the sand.

This is his happy place, his comfort zone. Did anyone tell him that I was going to be here today? Maybe that's why he decided to bail and not come. Maybe it was easier to just say something came up, then explaining to his parents why he didn't want me here.

A small knock on my window makes me jump, but when I look over and see Will standing there with a half dozen blow up rafts, I decide to jump out and help.

"You okay in there Len? You look like you might've just seen a ghost." Will smiles, showing off his perfectly white teeth. Being Grahams older brother, he's two years older than us and has basically walked around looking like a supermodel since I've known him. I don't think I ever saw Will without at least one girl draped over him, trying to be the one that finally got to be Will Thomas's girlfriend. I never really understood what the big deal was, why try to settle down a man who clearly didn't want to be settled down?

"Hey Will." I awkwardly laugh, "You know, it does kinda feel like I've seen a ghost, if I'm being honest. I haven't been here in so long. Do you need help with all of these rafts?"

"That would be great actually, the kids seem to think their old dad here can just handle everything. My guess, they're probably already out swimming. Let's head out back, my parents have been talking about you since Graham mentioned you being back in town."

I follow Will around the side of the house and into the backyard that holds so many memories for me. I wonder what Graham said when he told them I was back in town. Did he seem excited or was it just a mention in passing kind of thing?

"You've got that look on your face again Lennox. Stop overthinking all of this."

He nudges me with his elbow as we descend down the hill to the boathouse and beach area. "Hey guys, look who I found."

They all turn in our direction, and I meet the eyes of the family that I thought would one day be my family. The people who treated me like I was one of their own, never once looking down on me or my parents for not even being able to afford this boathouse, let alone everything else that comes along with it.

Catherine comes rushing over and pulls me into her arms, "Lennox dear, you are even more beautiful than the last time I saw you. And your mother says you just made junior partner at the law firm you've been at in New York. We're so proud of you."

"Give the girl a chance to breathe Cat, you are going to scare her away and we just got her back." Ed walks up alongside his wife and puts his arm around my shoulders, leaning in to kiss me on top of my head. "But she's right you know, we are so proud of you. Your parents kept us updated while you were away at school. Top of your class at Columbia, one of the youngest junior partners

Simion & Clark has ever had. Proud doesn't even cover it."

My cheeks start to blush, "Thank you. I have definitely been career driven for the past eleven years."

I take a moment to really take in these two. Catherine's once long, wavy, blonde hair is now shoulder length with a more natural blonde tone than before. But other than that, I don't think she's aged a bit. And Ed, other than his now salt and pepper hair, he's still the same tan, fit man with his piercing blue eyes that he passed down to his three children, as he was before.

Will walks over, picking up the floats I dropped when I was suddenly bear hugged by his mother. "You two going to share her with the rest of us? Come on, let's go down by the lake, the kids have something they wanted to show you all."

"Whose kids?" I ask.

"Mine." Will points out to the end of the dock where there are two children who look to be around the same age playing. "Those two crazy kids are mine, Sophia and Oliver. In case the toe heads and sky blue eyes didn't give them away, wait until you hang out for awhile, their mother claims they act just like me too."

I look around, but the only people here besides the ones I've already talked to are Halee, Luke, and baby Lauren, who are at the end of the dock with the other kids. "Is your wife inside the house?"

His father scuffles from the grill and Will shoots him a look. "She isn't here. We are... well, we're actually not together right now."

Ed says something under his breath that sounds a lot like "tramp" and Catherine slaps him in the arm on the way by.

Just as I am about to change the subject I hear a voice behind me that I wasn't expecting to hear today. "Hi family." When I finally turn around I find a shirtless Graham standing next to a beautiful blonde woman who looks like she fits in perfectly with this family.

"I-I didn't think you were going to be here." I stutter out.

"You didn't think I would be at my own family's cookout, so you thought maybe you would come in my place?" His voice is firm, angry like.

Halee walks up with Lauren in her hands, "Oh don't be an ass Graham, you did say that you couldn't come, and mom and dad have been wanting to see Lenny. Don't get your briefs in a twist."

"Language." Catherine takes the baby from Halee. "Huh, sweet pea. They may choose to talk like sailors but that doesn't mean you need to grow up thinking it's okay."

"Hello, I'm Emma. You must be Lennox, it's so great to finally meet you." She steps forward, holding her hand out. I reach to shake it while glancing over in Graham's direction who for the first time ever, looks like he might be panicking.

"It's so nice to meet you. And congratulations on the engagement."

Why was that word so hard for me to spit out. Engagement. Graham is engaged, and she's obviously perfect, perfect hair, perfect teeth, perfect tan skin with light freckles covering her nose, and her perfect polite southern accent. "I should head home. My mom said dad had a rough night and now that I think about it, I should be there to help in case it gets to be too much."

Halee sets her hand on my arm, "Please don't leave." Pleading with her eyes for some unknown reason, like she has a hidden agenda. "My parents are so excited to see you and catch up. Just stay."

Graham storms past us, heading to the fridge in the boathouse to grab a beer. "Anyone else?" He holds it up, before opening and taking a huge chug.

"Food's ready." Ed hollers.

♡♡♡

Dinner was a disaster, that mostly consisted of everyone asking about my life in New York, and Graham shooting daggers at me from the other end of the table. I should have left, I know this. But part of me wanted to be here, to somehow stake my claim on this place and these people. They were mine first. But the adult inside of me knows that's not true. They were never mine, they're his, and me being here is obviously too much for him. Too much for me.

But if I would have left, I wouldn't be sitting at the edge of this dock, alone, with my feet dangling in the warm July water, watching the orange hues take over the once blue sky.

I feel the dock move slightly before I hear anything. "Mind if I sit?" Her southern drawl sounds a lot like Luke's in so many ways, only hers is more sweet.

I turn, look up and smile, "Not at all."

Lie.

I do mind. What could we possibly have to talk about?

"Thank you. It's so beautiful up here. I try to remind myself of this right here, when I start to dread the Michigan winters y'all have." She giggles. Lord, even her giggle is perfect.

"Winters can be rough, but just think of all the different seasons you get to have up here. Summer is great, obviously." I wave my arm in the direction of the lake. "But fall, wait until you experience your first color change here. Apple picking, bonfires, warm apple cider, hayrides, it's the best. I'm sure you will love it. It's Graham's - "

I stop myself, suddenly not sure why I felt the need to try to convince Emma that moving here is the right thing for her. Maybe it's because I know *she* is what's best for the man we both love. The quiet between us is a deafening loud. There are so many questions we both want to ask, but both afraid of what we might find out if we ask them.

She breaks the silence first. "I've known about you for awhile now."

Her words surprised me. "I guess I don't know what you mean?"

Emma looks down at the ripples her moving feet are making in the calm waters. "A few months back I was packing up the house we lived in back home, and I found a box in the back of his closet that looked like it was ten-plus years old. He was running to the store to get more boxes because we ran out, so I was alone for awhile, and I decided to snoop. I know it's wrong, I was raised better, but I just had never seen it before and if he kept something this old looking, it must have something important to him or of value inside."

We both stare out into the clear water, "What was in the box?" I ask, but I have a feeling I already know.

"You." She pauses, holds her left hand out a little, adjusting her also perfect ring. "You were in the box Lennox. Pictures, movie stubs, notes, and then there were the letters."

I snap my head in her direction, only to find her looking right back at me. "What letters?"

"He wrote you." She breaks our eye contact and continues her admiration of the sunset. "I only read a few before I heard the truck door shut in the garage, but from the looks of it, he wrote you a lot after he joined the Army."

"Did you ask him about them? Or - " I clear my throat. "Me?"

"No. I put everything back in the box and placed it exactly where I found it. The next day, curiosity got the best of me, and I went back to read more, but the box was gone. The man who wrote you those, I've never met him."

"Emma, you're engaged to him."

"No. I'm not. The man I'm marrying hasn't let me in like he spoke on those pages. I've known since we met that something or someone hurt him. I knew he wasn't whole, but I wanted to be the one to put him back together again. He's brave, strong, and one of the best people I've ever met, but he's not complete. Something is missing, and after finding that box, I wondered if you were the missing piece, but I wasn't sure until tonight."

"Tonight?! Emma, there is nothing between Graham and I anymore."

Lie.

Apparently I'm just going to continue to lie my way through this night.

"I'm glad you feel that way because I love that man with everything I have. I believe that he was made for me…"

I swallow, trying to hold back the pain of hearing another woman profess her love for the man who has consumed me since I was sixteen.

"…and even though I may never be his person, I know that he's mine."

And there it is.

She's not walking away from him like I did all those years ago, instead she's going to stay and fight for what they have, for their future, just like I should have done. And Graham deserves to be fought for, he deserves to have someone who isn't a total train wreck and can complete him in a way I never could.

"I think you're exactly what he needs Emma."

And surprisingly, I don't have to choke those words out because deep down, I know they're the truth.

Chapter 9

Graham

My past and future are colliding right in front of me and there's nothing I can do about it. When Emma called me this morning and said she was surprising me by flying in for a few days, I told my parents that I wouldn't be able to make it to the family cookout. I assumed that she would want to spend some time alone, considering it's been a couple of months since we've seen each other. But after I picked her up from the airport, she insisted it would be great to see everyone, and today's cookout would be the perfect opportunity to see them all at one time.

So we stopped at the house to drop off her suitcase, changed into our bathing suits and headed this way. Leaving us with zero time to even look in the direction of the other, let alone achieve any intimacy. I've never been more grateful for being in a hurry in my life. After that kiss with Lennox last night, which nearly set my entire body on fire, my mind is spinning and I don't know what to think.

Emma is everything I thought I needed in life. She made me feel like I wasn't missing a part of myself anymore. Things with us are great, we don't fight, the sex is good, it's almost like we were made for each other. But then I think about how a single kiss with Lennox can make me feel things again that I've longed to feel for years, and it makes me question everything Emma and I have.

How can I be in love with her, but still have these immense, ground shaking feelings whenever I'm around Lenny? How do I move forward and start a life with this incredible woman who deserves the world, knowing that I already gave it all to someone else?

"What's going through that thick skull of yours big brother?" Halee walks out onto the deck that overlooks the docks and lake, hands me a fresh beer and takes a long sip of her white wine.

"What do you think they are talking about down there?" I nod in the direction of the only two women who have ever owned a piece of my heart.

"Well, if I had to guess, maybe they're comparing notes and deciding who has to be stuck with your grumpy butt for the rest of time."

When I don't say anything she bumps me with her shoulder, "I'm just kidding. Why do you seem so worried about them talking?"

"I kissed Lennox last night."

The words just fall out of my mouth. I didn't have any intention of telling anyone about the kiss, except Emma. As much as I don't want to hurt her, I know telling her what happened is the right thing to do. I look over at my sister who just has a smile on her face, "You going to say something?"

She turns and looks at me, "What do you want me to say? Should I scold you, yell at you, tell you that you're a shitty person? Because I don't believe that to be true."

"How can you say that Halee? I am engaged to marry another woman in two months and last night I took Lenny to a spot that I knew could bring up feelings between us and in a moment of weakness, I kissed her. I can't even blame her for it, I leaned over and put my lips on hers. And the shitty part is, after I pulled away, after

I realized what I was doing and how wrong it was, I
wanted to do it again."

"But did you?" I raise my eyebrows at her,
but don't answer. "Did you kiss her again Graham,
after you realized how wrong it was?"

"No."

"Did kissing her feel right?"

"How could it be right when I have Emma?"

"That's not what I'm asking you Graham.
When you and Lenny kissed, putting aside the fact
that you are set to marry Emma, did it feel right?"

"Yes."

I know that shouldn't be my answer, but it
is. Nothing in that moment felt wrong, if anything it
was the most right I've felt since the day I stepped
on that bus, handing my life over to the Army.

"I think you are in a hard spot big brother.
And maybe you need to take a long look at your life
and who you want to spend it with."

"Halee, Emma and I are getting married in
two months. Right here in this backyard. The invites

have already been sent out, caterers have been paid, all the T's have been crossed and the I's dotted. It doesn't matter what I want, there is no way I could ever disappoint Emma like that."

She rolls her eyes and turns her attention back to the sunset, while sipping her wine. It annoys me how much she resembles that stupid Kermit the Frog that's always sipping his tea. "You know Graham, for a badass hero who earned a Purple Heart, because he's so brave and quick to react to unexpected situations, you're kind of an idiot. Go ahead, let the love of your life slip away again and marry the girl, who doesn't make the ground you are standing on shake when you kiss her. If you are okay with spending the rest of your life with someone other than your soulmate, then that's on you."

♡♡♡

"Tonight was fun. I'm glad we went." Emma smiles at me as we crawl into bed. After her and Lennox spent about thirty minutes out on the dock together, Lenny came up and thanked everyone for a fun evening and went home. We left shortly after, making the quick drive around the lake to our house.

"Me too." I lean over and press my lips to her forehead before laying back on my pillow. "There's something I need to talk to you about."

She climbs on top of my lap, straddling her legs around my hips and places her core directly on my dick. "Maybe we can talk later? It's been so long Graham." She begins to pepper light kisses along my jaw, slowly working her way down my neck and across my abs.

I stop her by lifting her chin, so our eyes meet. "I think maybe this is a talk we should have before this goes any further."

She moves off of me and sits cross-legged on the other side of the bed. "Oh God, you're worrying me Graham."

I struggle to find the words to explain what happened with Lennox and me. I know I'm going to have to answer a bunch of questions about the two of us, and frankly I'm not exactly ready to make this stroll down memory lane. Especially with my soon-to-be wife.

"Babe, say something. You're freaking me out."

Fuck it, better to just rip the bandaid off. Right? "I kissed Lennox."

She sucks in a deep breath, but doesn't look as hurt or surprised as I expected. "Is that all that happened?"

Is she serious right now? I just told my fiancé that I kissed another woman that wasn't her and that's all she has to say to me?

"Yes. We only kissed, and it was only one time."

"When?"

"It happened last night. She went out with all the girls and when she brought Halee home she was just going to walk back to her parents, but I said that was crazy and I would give her a ride. She mentioned how the stars here were something she missed, that she couldn't see them in the city and it made her sad. So I took her to the baseball practice fields and - "

She holds up her hand to stop me, "I don't need the details. I just need to know if it's something you plan on letting happen again?"

How do I answer that? I didn't plan on it happening last night but it did, and just an hour ago I told my sister how it didn't feel wrong. But this is Emma, the woman who stood by me when I came back from overseas after seeing my closest friend take his last breath in my arms, because I wasn't quick enough getting to him. She's the one who wakes me up when I'm having nightmares and talks me off the ledge, holding me until I fall back asleep. This woman is uprooting her entire life to move hours away from the only home she has ever known, because she knows it's what I need to heal. She deserves me at my best, and she definitely doesn't deserve me kissing my ex.

Her hand cups my cheek, "Graham, it's an easy question. Was this a closure thing, or is this that door opening back up? You and I can't move forward with our lives if that door is still open. I'm willing to look past this and forget it ever happened, but I need you to look me in the eyes and tell me you still *want* to marry me."

I lean forward and press my lips to hers. "I love you Emma. And I can't wait to marry you."

Chapter 10

Lennox

It's my birthday.

The big three-zero. And as much as I want to stay in bed, dwelling on the fact that my world seems to be crumbling around me, Halee and Quinn have insisted we go out.

I don't know the details, except to dress up and be at Stubs at eight. So here I am, sitting in my car, with ten minutes to spare, dreading the idea of going inside this bar. Who have they invited? Is it just a girls night or will the guys be here too? Better question, will Graham be here… with Emma?

After meeting Emma two weeks ago, I left the Thomas house, and made myself a promise that I had to move forward with my life. As much as it terrifies me, I have to put myself out there, try to be open to meeting someone, and just have fun.

I've spent way too long looking backward, letting the things that happened to me control my future. And that ends tonight. I will let loose, I will have a few drinks and maybe I will even dance with a complete stranger who I'll never see again.

The new Lennox Coleman starts now. Well as soon as I can force myself out of this damn car and into the bar I've walked into more times than I can count.

"Surprise!" The large group of people yell from the back corner when I enter the side door.

Halee comes skipping over and slinks her arm through mine. "I hope it's okay, but I invited a few people."

"A few, Halee, do I even know all these people?"

She laughs, "No probably not, but how else am I going to convince you to stay in Iron City, if you don't make a bunch of new friends and fall back in love with our small town charm."

"Oh, I'm not moving back - "

She interrupts me by introducing everyone that I don't already know, "So you obviously already know Quinn, but this is her husband Walker. You've met Charlie and Annie at girls night, and I'm sure you remember JR, but this is one of the guys from the department, we all call him Mack."

Mack stands up from the booth he was just sitting in and walks towards me with his hand extended. He's tall, maybe not as tall as Graham but at least six-two. He has short medium brown hair, cleanly shaven, and from what I can tell zero tattoos. The complete opposite of the man that has been invading my dreams for as long as I can remember. Maybe the opposite is a good thing, it could be exactly what I need to get myself back out there.

"Zac MacKenzie, but as you heard, most people call me Mack." He brings my hand up to his mouth and places a tender kiss on the top of it.

"It's great to meet you Zac, thanks for coming tonight."

"Absolutely. Can I get you a drink?" I hesitate for a minute, knowing that in the past my answer would always be "no". How can I stay in complete control of any situation if I start drinking? But not tonight, tonight the answer needs to be "yes".

"I would love a drink actually."

About three margaritas in, my face is starting to feel a little fuzzy, but I think I like it. I've been so in control for so long that it feels good to let my hair down and feel free for once. I'm talking with Charlie about her son Tucker when I feel someone come up behind me, brushing my hair off one shoulder, pressing his lips to my ear.

Zac.

"Wanna dance, hot stuff?"

Suddenly feeling even more unlike myself, I turn so our bodies are still touching and look up into his eyes, "I thought you'd never ask."

He takes my cup from my hand, setting it down on the table next to Charlie and pulls me towards the dance floor, where a song is playing that I've never heard before. But I don't let that stop me. Instead, I sway my hips to the beat, falling deep into the rhythm of the music and the man grinding behind me.

The new Lennox Coleman seems to be working out just fine.

Chapter 11

Graham

I told myself I wasn't coming here tonight, but here I am. After the kiss with Lennox, and then spending the next five days ironing out wedding plans and reconnecting with Emma, I came to realize distance is what I need. I can't go around kissing Lenny, if I'm nowhere near her.

But again, here I am.

When Halee texted this morning and said if I was bored I should stop out to Stubs for Lennox's thirtieth birthday, I laughed. I don't know what kind of hidden agenda my baby sister has, but she seems to be stuck on this whole soulmate thing, since meeting Luke, and now she is hell-bent on proving that Lennox is it for me.

What could go wrong? We are going to be in a packed bar, with everyone we know, there is no way I'm going to make some dumbass decision like kissing her, in front of these people. As long as Lennox and I aren't alone, we should be able to coexist.

After my eyes adjust to the darkness, I do what I always do, assess my surroundings. A solider always knows where all the exits are, in case of an emergency. But when my eyes move over the dance floor I see something I didn't expect; Lennox grinding all over another man, a man whose hands are touching places they shouldn't be.

"What the fuck is that?" I say out loud to no one in particular.

Halee looks over at me, "Hey big bro, I thought you said you weren't coming?"

"Who the hell is she dancing with?"

My eyes still fixed on the two of them on the dance floor, the way her hands are gripping his neck, and his hands.

Before I can even begin to understand whats happening, the anger inside of me boils over and I find myself rushing in the direction of the dance floor. I push him off of her, causing Lennox to fall back into a couple dancing close by.

"What the hell dude, what's your problem?" The punk shouts over the music, puffing his chest out like he's going to do something. I smile at him, daring him to make a move, knowing I could destroy this guy in two seconds, if given the chance.

Lennox steps between us, placing her back up against the other guy, as if she is "with him".

"Graham, what are you doing?"

"What am I doing? What the hell are you doing Lennox? You were standing in the middle of the dance floor of a crowded bar, grinding on this guy. Have you been drinking?"

"Do you know this guy?" Punk boy speaks.

"Yeah, she knows me. I'm her - "

Lenny's face falls and her eyes turn from angry to sympathetic. A hand falls on my shoulder causing me to jump, "Easy man, it's just me. JR. Why don't we go to the bar and get something to drink?"

My eyes don't leave hers. What was I going to just say? I'm her what? Her ex? The guy who made love to her under the stars for the first time, the guy who promised her forever, the guy who thought he would be marrying *her*, not someone else.

"Yeah, a drink sounds good."

"Four shots of Tennessee Fire," I shout to the bartender over the crowd. "And whatever this guy wants." Nodding my head in the direction of JR.

"I'll just have a Bud Light draft, thanks." JR turns to me. "Four shots huh, you think that's really a good idea Graham?"

"Who the fuck are you, the drink police? I'm thirty-years-old, I know how many damn shots I can have. And if I'm going to sit here and watch this shit all night, I need something to take the edge off before I start snapping necks."

The bartender sets my shots and JR's draft in front of us and walks away. "Graham, what the hell was that about anyway? You acted as if that was your girl out there dancing on another guy."

"That is my girl!" I say a little louder than I planned, causing multiple people to turn and look at me. I quickly slam the rest of my shots.

"Oh yeah? So what exactly does that make Emma?"

I run my hands through my now shoulder length hair, I should probably get it cut before the wedding. Emma hates it this long, even though she would never say those words out loud. "Emma is... Emma, it's completely different man."

"My mom used to tell me all the time, 'You can't have your cake and eat it too'. Sounds an awful lot like you are trying to have both. I don't really know Lennox or Emma all that well, but neither of them really seem like the sister wives type." He shrugs his shoulders and turns his attention to the baseball game on the TV in front of us.

"Yeah... you wanna start giving love advice out Romeo? How about the fact that you are head over heels in love with your best friend, but she has your ass stuck in the friend zone."

His shoulders bounce slightly as he laughs, "Charlie and I are complicated, that's for sure. But at least in my case, the only heart I'm breaking, is my own in the long run. From where I'm sitting, you're going to hurt one of them if you keep on the same road you're on now. It's obvious both of those women love you. The question is, which one do you love?"

Lennox doesn't love me, she couldn't possibly love me anymore. Right? We haven't seen each other in almost twelve years, how could she still be in love with me after all this time?

I turn back to the crowd just in time to see Lenny stumble into the booth where Charlie and Quinn are sitting across the room; she's drunk.

I throw a couple twenties on the bar and slap JR on the shoulder, "Thanks for the talk man, but I think I'm going to go offer to take Lennox home." *Before the other guy does.* I say the last part to myself.

JR smiles and shakes his head, "Whatever man. I think that's a terrible idea, but you aren't going to listen to me anyway." He hollers as I walk away.

When I reach the booth, the dipshit from the dance floor is sitting next to Lennox with his arm resting around her shoulders. Her eyes find mine, "You ready to go home Lenny?"

"Home?"

"Yeah, I think it's time I take you home."

"I got her dude." The punk says, pulling her closer into his chest.

Without breaking eye contact with her I respond, "I got her. You ready sweet lips?"

The left side of her mouth curls up, showing off her adorable dimple. "Yeah, I'm ready." She slides from under dipshits arm and slips out of the booth. Stumbling.

About two minutes after getting into my truck the magnitude of this hits me at once, just how bad of an idea this is. I all but had to carry her out of that damn bar, and having her so close, hearing her drunken mumbles, basically crumbled what's left of the wall around my heart.

"Please don't take me home. Take me anywhere but home. I can't deal with that reality tonight Graham cracker." Her words slur as she says them, but I can still hear the pain.

"Do you want to just drive around for awhile before I drop you off?"

"Sleep, I need sleep." She mumbled before she lays across the seat, resting her tired, intoxicated head on my lap.

I run my fingers through the caramel ends of her hair, "I got you Lenny. Just go to sleep."

Next thing I know I'm carrying the woman I told myself not to be alone with, into my empty house, up the stairs and into the spare bedroom. I lay her down, remove her shoes, and pull the blankets up around her, then force myself to walk out of the room and into my own.

"What the fuck are you thinking?!" I say out loud to myself.

This is a bad idea. Probably even worse than taking her to the damn baseball fields, but I guess making poor choices is my thing lately when it comes to Lennox Coleman.

I strip down to my briefs and grab my phone out of my pants pocket, noticing a text from Emma as I plug it in.

Emma: Hey babe. Hope you had a good night out. Mom and I went to a vineyard today and the heat got to me, so I'm going to pass out

early. I will call you when I wake up. I love you, and I can't wait to be your wife in 42 days.

I set my phone down. God, I'm a piece of shit. What would Emma think if she knew there was another woman in our home? And not just any woman, my own version of kryptonite. The one person in this world who could bring me to my knees at the mere sight of her.

I moan in frustration as I lay down and force my eyes closed.

This is no big deal, Lennox and I are friends. And this is what friends do for each other, they take care of one another when they are too drunk, or when they need to avoid going home. I would do the same thing for any of my other friends.

Only difference, I wouldn't want my body entangled with any of my other friends.

This is going to be a long night.

Chapter 12

Graham

I wake up to the familiar noise of someone screaming. Only this time, it isn't me.

Lennox.

I jump out of bed and sprint in the direction of the spare room, and find her flailing her arms and legs, screaming words I struggle to understand.

I flip on the light and run over to her. "Lenny, baby, stop."

"Don't, please, don't touch me." She screams, her eyes still squeezed tight.

"Lennox it's me, it's Graham. Wake up, you're having a bad dream."

"Please don't do this, please." A single tear cascades down her cheek.

"It's Graham. You are safe Lenny. You're safe and I'm right here."

Her eyes open wide, and she sits up, pulling the sheet up around her body. "Graham?"

I move up closer to her, keeping enough distance to be safe, but knowing she needs to be comforted right now. "You're safe. I think you were having a bad dream."

"Yeah. Just a dream." She tries to sound relieved but something in her voice seems off. Like this is something that has happened before.

"Do you have bad dreams a lot? You kept saying things like 'don't touch me'. Has someone touched you before without your permission?" She looks away, and then slides her body back down so her head's on the pillow. "Lennox - "

"Just lay with me." She interrupts me. "Please, until I fall back asleep. We don't have to touch, but just knowing you're in here will be comforting. I'm sorry I woke you."

"Don't be sorry Len, but can we talk about what just happened?"

"Not tonight. I just want to go back to sleep. Tomorrow." Her words drift off and her sleepy eyes fall shut.

I get up and walk across the room to turn off the lights and her head lifts up, "You're leaving?"

I hit the switch and walk back to the bed, crawling in next to her, bringing our bodies dangerously close. "No sweet lips, I'm not leaving you."

She rolls to her side, sliding her body closer to mine, and I do exactly what I shouldn't and wrap my arm around her waist, pulling her in tighter. In this moment I feel even closer to her than I did mere hours ago. Something happened in her life that causes her enough pain to have to relive it in her dreams, I know that pain firsthand. I have to relive watching my best friends blood cover my arms and legs as he says his last words and takes his last breath.

Lennox's breathing calms and her once tense body relaxes. I can tell she is sleeping but nothing in me wants to get up and move to my own bed. This feels like exactly where I need to be, and just as I start to drift to sleep, the words I have longed to hear for years, hit me like a freight train.

"I love you, Graham."

Chapter 13

Lennox

I wake to a warm strong arm draped over my stomach, and instantly think back to last night and the dancing that happened with Zac. But when I look to my left, I see the long blonde hair and torso covered in tattoos, the night flashes back through my mind.

The drinks, the dancing, the almost fight, Graham bringing me here, and my nightmare, which led to us in the same bed. Him being basically naked.

I know I should slip out and leave before he wakes, saving us both from the awkwardness that is bound to come when he wakes up, but I can't. I don't want to leave this bed, or him. I want to beg him to pick me, choose me. Call off his wedding with Emma and make love to me under the stars like he did so many times when we were younger. But I know that's not a fair expectation to have. It would make all of this so much easier to give in to if she was some terrible person who didn't deserve him, but she isn't. She is exactly who I would pick for him at the end of the day.

The Army was good to him. The tattoos, the muscles, the cockiness that drips out of him with everything he says or does. Eighteen-year-old Graham was hot, but thirty-year-old Graham is sex on a stick.

As he lays on his stomach, the sheet dips just below the waistband of his briefs, giving me a perfect view of the two dimples that sit right above them. The firm muscles across his back and shoulders are perfectly covered in various tattoos that make me want to trace my fingers along them, getting reacquainted with every inch of the body I used to know so well.

I lose the battle of temptation and my fingertip maneuvers its way along the tribal symbols that cover the arm that is laying across me.

He slowly turns his head so his face is towards me and his eyes open. I expect him to jump out of bed and run in the opposite direction now that it's daylight.

But he doesn't. Instead, he smiles that perfect Graham smile. "Mornin'."

I giggle. "Good morning."

He rolls over to his back and stretches his arms above his head, displaying his massive morning wood. "What's so funny?"

I look away, "Well I was laughing because I was sure you were going to run away after realizing who you were in bed with. But now it's just weird because of…" I point in the direction of his junk.

"Oh that guy, apparently he is just as excited to wake up next to you as I am."

I sigh, and throw my arm over my face. "You can't say things like that."

"I know. But I can't help it. I don't understand my feelings anymore. Two months ago, everything was so black and white. I was getting married, and now, everything is grey. Seeing you, and having you back in my life again wasn't expected and I definitely wasn't prepared for it. It shook me seeing you again. And now I don't know what I want."

"Graham…"

"I know Lenny. Trust me, I know. But I have to say these things, if I don't get them off my chest I feel like I will explode."

"But it's not fair. It's not fair to Emma, it's not fair to me, and it's definitely not fair to you. I'm broken Graham, and Emma isn't. She is able to be your rock in rough waters, and I don't think I can be that person anymore. I'm not the same girl you were in love with forever ago, things change, I changed."

"Does this have anything to do with the nightmare last night?"

"No." Lie. "Okay, maybe… yes. But I really can't talk about it."

He turns so he is on his side, facing me, head propped up on his hand. That's when I notice the single tattoo that covers the left side of his chest. Without thinking I reach out and begin to trace the giant set of lips that look like they are covered in candy. "It was my first tattoo."

"Is it - " My words fade away and the tears begin to blur my vision.

"It's you, sweet lips. I got it as soon as I got out of basic. You've always been right here with me." He lifts his hand, placing it over the tattoo covering his heart. "Not a day has gone by in the past twelve years that I haven't thought about you. About what I left behind when I chose to get on the bus that day and not stay and fight for us. I wouldn't take back my time in the military, I loved what I did and what it represented, but I would change so much Lenny. I have loved you since you walked into that gym class, wearing that terrible Matchbox Twenty T-shirt all those years ago, and I will love you until the day I die."

I wipe away the tears, and his hand catches mine, pulling me on top of him, so I'm straddling his legs. Still only wearing my dress from the night before, his semi-erect penis presses hard into my core, warming me from the inside out. Leaning forward, I run both hands through his long, unruly bedhead, and bring my face down to his.

I know this is wrong, but it feels so right. And when his lips meet mine I feel the energy zip all the way down to my toes. His hands roaming up and down my thighs as he moves me back and forth on top of him.

His body freezes when the sound of his phone in another room breaks up our electrifying make out session.

"Fuck" Graham picks me up and sets me down on the bed, then jumps up and jogs off to wherever the sound is coming from.

I take a moment to really take in my surroundings since from the minute my eyes opened all I could do was stare at the man lying next to me. I open the slider that leads out to a deck area overlooking the same lake his parents and sister live on. The lake we all grew up swimming, tubing and making memories on.

"What are you doing to me Lenny?" His voice startles me back to reality. I turn to find him leaning against the door frame, still shirtless but now wearing a pair of sweatpants.

"What do you mean?"

His hands uncross from his chest and make their way through his hair that I've come to love long over the past few weeks. He lets out a long sigh and then moves towards me, both of us turning to look back at the lake.

"I mean, I'm not this man." He stops, like he's carefully thinking out how he wants to word his next sentence. "I'm loyal to a fault Len, you know that. But when it comes down to the two of you, I have a hard time figuring out who I'm supposed to be loyal to. I love her, there's no doubt about that in my mind. But will I ever love her like I loved you?"

The word *loved* shoots a pain through my heart.

I go to speak but he continues, "I came to your house that morning before I got on the bus. I needed to see you, to tell you that no matter what happened, we would always find a way to make things work. But when your mom told me you didn't want to see me, it destroyed me from the inside out. From that moment on, nothing that happened to me, at basic training, or otherwise, could be any worse than the pain I felt knowing you didn't want me anymore."

Oh god. I have to stop him, he has to know that I did want him. That I was coming to that stupid going away party that night to tell him exactly that. But am I ready to tell him the reason I didn't make it? And if I tell him, will he find out what happened to me in the months following that night? Part of me wants to tell him, but the other part of me knows that if he finds out, it will haunt him the same way it haunts me and my mom. And I don't want that for him, there is nothing he could have done back then to stop it, and there's definitely nothing that can be done now.

"I let you go Lenny. At least that's what I told myself. I pushed you to the back of my mind, and tried like hell to move forward without you. And I did move forward, I had lots of meaningless hookups with women who would temporarily fill the Lennox shaped hole in my heart. But at the end of the day, I was still a shell of a man. Until I met Emma. I was at a bar with a bunch of the guys, and my buddy picked her out of the crowd to be my next conquest. So in true Graham fashion I walked up and handed her one of my cheesy pickup lines that probably sounded a lot like 'you wanna get outta here', which worked for all the past women. But not Emma. She turned and looked into my broken eyes, smiled, and said 'No, but I would love to have a drink with you and talk'. And that's all that we did for months, we talked about anything and everything…"

Me? Did he talk about me? The question is on the tip of my tongue, but I don't have to ask.

"…except you. The other night when she acted like she's heard all about you, she hasn't. Her and I have never spoken about you Lenny."

I stop him before he can shatter my heart anymore, "She told me she found a box. A box full of me."

He smiles, still facing the lake. "Of course she did, and because she's Emma, she never said anything."

"Where's the box now? She said there were letters inside it."

"It's gone. I burned it." And just like that, my insides crumble. He gave up on us. "We were packing up the rest of our house in South Carolina and I decided that it was time. If I was going to marry her, I needed to let you go. I finally felt a closure that I was searching for all of those years, but then here you come, waltzing back into Iron City. It's almost like you knew I was letting go, so you had to show back up and destroy me again."

Tears fall down my face, I angrily turn and face him. "Graham, I'm here because my dad is dying. Trust me when I say, being in this town, and this close to you, dredging up memories that I have tried for years to move on from, is not exactly what I wanted. I have a good life back in New York, I have a career that challenges me every day, and amazing friends."

"How about a guy?" He interrupts me.

"What?"

"You were talking about your fabulous life in the big city, but you didn't mention a guy. Is there one? Are you being just as unfaithful and cruel to someone else as I am to Emma?"

"Would that make you feel better? Knowing that I have this amazing, perfect man back in New York and yet I can't seem to stay away from you?" I wait for his reply but it doesn't come. "No, Graham, there is no one else."

"But there has been, right?"

Chapter 14

Graham

I don't know why I just asked her that. Of course there have been other guys, it's been almost twelve years since we've been together. I would need both hands, both feet and someone else's hands to count the women I've been with over the years. Not that I'm proud of that, but it's the truth. For a while there, I was just your basic man whore, sleeping my way through all the uniform chasers that hung out in the bars around base.

"Have I dated? Sure, I've gone on a few dates here and there." Her voice is quiet, almost as if she is suddenly shy.

"But it's been over a decade and you're, as of yesterday, thirty-years-old. You've for sure had other - lovers, right?"

Why am I asking her this?

"Um, well honestly, I spent most of my time devoted to being in the top of my class and then when I graduated I jumped right into work. You don't become a junior partner at my age without working your ass off. That doesn't leave much time for relationships, and I'm not really a one night stand kind of girl. You should know that."

I turn and pull her so we are facing each other, "Sweet lips, am I the last person you've had sex with?"

Her whole body freezes and she turns, heading back inside the house. "Yeah, something like that."

I follow her into the room where she is gathering up all of her belongings quickly. "What are you doing? You can't just drop a bomb like that and then leave Lenny. You're seriously telling me no man has been inside of you since me?"

"What does it matter Graham?" Unshed tears threaten her glossy eyes. "Would that change anything? You are getting married, to seriously one of the best people I think I've ever met, and here we are. Doing whatever the hell it is we are doing. We said we wanted to be friends but I think this is the proof we needed, us being 'just friends' isn't possible. I need to leave, and you need to let me leave."

I know she's right. But I'm not ready to let her go. Hell, I don't know if I will ever again be okay with just letting her go. Especially now that I know I'm the only man in this world who knows what it feels like to be inside of her, and how magical it truly feels.

"Lenny, I'm not ready to let you go."

She walks over, with her purse slung across her body, places both of her hands on either side of my face. "I know Graham, but you and I aren't meant to be together. She's good for you, let her be the good you need in your life. Emma is moving here in what, a week? She is uprooting everything she knows to follow you across the country and be with you. She's doing exactly what I wasn't willing to do all of those years ago. You are choosing the better woman, Graham, trust me. I come with a whole lot of baggage, and I could never give you what you need. Let me go."

Instantly I remember her nightmare. "Wait! Last night, you were crying out like someone was touching you when they shouldn't be, almost like they were hurting you."

She leans forward on her toes, pulling my face down to meet her halfway. "Goodbye, Graham cracker." And after she places a light kiss on the corner of my lips, Lennox Coleman walks out of my house, and possibly back out of my life.

Chapter 15

Graham

It's been three weeks since I've seen Lenny. I painfully watched her walk out of my house that day and she didn't look back. The first night I drove over to her parents house, planning on knocking on the door and screaming at her. Except I wasn't sure what I was supposed to say. I was angry, hell, I'm still angry. It's like she took the choice of what I wanted away, for the second time in our lives. She told me to be with Emma, she told me she isn't good for me, just like all those years ago when she told me that we wouldn't work out because we wanted such different things.

So when I pulled up in front of that cape cod style home that once housed the girl I fell in love with, I realized that girl doesn't live there anymore. She is now a woman whose life and dreams are back in New York and while she is currently here, eventually she will leave again. What we had wasn't enough to keep us together back then, and

I'm crazy to think it would be enough now. Too much time has passed. So I drove away.

"Hey babe, what are you doing up so early?" Emma's voice pulls me out of the fog. She has been here, in the home I purchased for us to share and start our life together for a little over two weeks. Shortly after she got here, her mom and younger sister arrived to help with all of the last minute wedding plans. The fact that they are staying in the room that not too long ago, Lennox and I spent the night in, eats me up.

I didn't tell Emma about that night - mostly because it wasn't going to change anything and I knew it would only cause her more pain. Pain that she doesn't deserve to feel. So I put that night, with all the other memories of Lennox and I, in a mental box and shoved it to the back of my head. Making a promise to myself that I would be a better man from now on.

My fiancé makes her way over to me, wearing an off the shoulder, oversized night shirt that would typically turn all of my gears. As she lifts one leg over mine to straddle me, I catch a glimpse of her naked core. But still, nothing happens. I convinced her when she came home that we should refrain from sex until our wedding night to make it more special, which she jumped at the romantic idea. Even though nothing about it was romantic in the least. Instead I'm just a man who is struggling to get a hard-on for his soon-to-be wife because his head's all stuffed up with thoughts of another woman.

"Graham." Emma places her hand on my cheek and pulls my attention to her. "What's going on? Where's your head at?"

I smile at the warmth in her eyes. Her concern is genuine, and her love for me is so strong and enduring. I don't deserve it, I don't deserve her.

"Nothing, just thinking about tonight, and tomorrow."

"Are you excited for a night out with the guys? It's your last hoorah as a free man, ya know." She lays a feather like kiss on my lips.

"Yeah, I'm excited. But part of me feels like this night is more about Will than it is about anyone else. He and JR planned this whole thing with the party bus, bar hopping and knowing them I'm sure there will be strippers. Honestly, I just don't feel up for it."

"You will have fun. And tomorrow, when you see me again, I will be the one in the white dress walking down the aisle towards you." She lets out a small squeal of excitement that makes the corner of my mouth curve up. She's so cute when she gets this way. "I'm going to be your wife tomorrow, you will be my husband. How crazy is that?"

"So crazy." She lays her head on my shoulder, legs still straddling me, while her arms are laced around my back. We sit like this for what seems like hours until her mom knocks on our bedroom door, telling Emma it's time for them to get around to head to their spa day.

"I love you." She whispers in my ear and she climbs off and heads into our master bathroom to take a shower.

♡♡♡

"Dude! Are you ready for tonight?" JR slaps me on the shoulder as we climb onto the party bus. I started in on the whiskey about twenty minutes after Emma, her mom, and sister left. So let's just say that I'm right around four hours and at least seven shots in at this point, and my focus on anything is definitely starting to fade.

"As ready as I'll ever be."

"And tomorrow? You ready for that baby brother?" Will asks as he pours us all shots of whatever poison he has chosen for the evening.

"As ready as I'll ever be."

All four heads turn in my direction - Will, JR, Luke and Walker stop whatever they're doing and wait, as if I need to say more.

"Ahhhh… I know Halee and I aren't married yet, but I feel like if the night before our wedding my words are 'as ready as I'll ever be' you are probably going to knock me on my ass. Aren't you excited?"

I sigh and run my fingers through my hair, which is now much shorter since I agreed to get it faded again for the wedding. "I am excited. I just have a lot on my mind these days. I'm kind of just ready to get tomorrow over with so we can start our life together, ya know?"

JR hands me the glass that Will poured, "And the thing or person on your mind, wouldn't happen to be about five-foot-six, with long brown hair and crazy intense brown eyes, would it?"

Walker looks around confused, "Wait, I thought Emma had blonde hair?"

JR's glare doesn't leave mine when he responds to Walker, "Lennox Coleman. The one that got away."

"Oh shit." Walker says quietly. "Quinn and I need to leave the house more. I swear I never know what's going on, I didn't even realize this was a thing."

"It's not a thing." I say through my clenched teeth at JR, "And I would appreciate it if my *friend,* and I say that term loosely, would stop saying it is."

Will laughs, "Oh it's most definitely a thing. You have been in love with that girl since your freshman year of high school. All it took was her walking back in and it resparked all those feelings you thought you put behind you. The real question is, have you put them behind you? Because trust me baby bro, you don't want to look back on your life five years from now and regret the decisions you made as you're signing your divorce papers."

I don't need this. The doubt that's been in my head since seeing Lenny at the salon all those weeks ago needs zero help surfacing. "What do you guys want me to say? Huh? That I don't love

Lenny and my whole heart will be with Emma tomorrow when we vow to love and cherish one another? I can't do that. I love Emma, enough to know that I can't hurt her. Lennox is just... Lennox. She comes in and changes everything and then walks away when she doesn't want to put forth the effort to make it work. I'm getting married tomorrow, to Emma, and in a few weeks Lenny will go back to the Big Apple and forget all about me again."

"But will you forget about her?" Luke asks. "I'm just saying, I have a pretty good idea of what it feels like when the person you love walks away or in my case, forces you to walk away. That pain and emptiness doesn't just disappear no matter how much you try to mask it. Just think about what you're doing man, it's not too late to make this right."

"What the fuck is this, a therapy session? I thought this was my bachelor party, bring on the booze, bars, and bad decisions."

Chapter 16

Lennox

As I walk into the kitchen, the first thing that jumps out to me is the front page of the Iron City newspaper. *Local hero marries southern belle this weekend.* "Ugh" I drop it in the wastebasket on my way to the coffee machine.

"Sorry Lenny," my mom gives me a sympathetic look as she enters the kitchen behind me. "I meant to throw that away this morning. How are you holding up?"

Ha. That's the question of the year apparently. Between the phone calls and texts from my colleagues and friends back in New York who are worried about how my dad is doing, and then the girls here, concerned about the upcoming wedding. I can't seem to catch a break to truly gauge how I am feeling these days.

"I'm okay momma, thank you."

She sits next to me at the kitchen island and hands me the sugar and creamer. "Are you really okay? You seem to just be existing these days. And up until a few weeks ago, I felt like you had that spark of excitement for life back in your eyes that I haven't seen in a long time. Have you thought anymore about the invitation to go to the wedding?"

I laugh again, but this time it is actually out loud. "That invite was just her final way of staking her claim on him. She doesn't want me at that wedding anymore than he does, and Lord knows I don't want to be there. What happens when it gets to the part where they ask if anyone objects? And then there I am, standing in the middle of his parents backyard screaming 'don't do it' like we are in some Lifetime movie."

This time it's her turn to giggle, which is a sound I don't hear out of my tired and stressed mom much these days. "I actually don't think they do that anymore, at least outside of the movies. But I understand. I also thought it was strange that she showed up here wanting to chat with you."

"Good morning Mrs. Coleman. I was actually hoping to talk to Lennox for a minute if she has the time?"

I hear the voice coming from the front door but I still stand frozen in the hallway. What could she possibly be doing here right now? I knew from my chat with Halee last night that she was due back in town any day now to start the final preparations for the wedding, but having the perfect Emma Collins standing on my front step was not something I was expecting.

I walk around the corner and place my hand on my mom's shoulder. "Momma, pops just fell asleep, but he was able to get down a few sips of water before passing out. I wrote it down on the notebook, but I wanted to let you know. I'm going to go for a walk with Emma if you are okay with being alone for awhile."

"Thank you sweetie, and absolutely. I think I will take a book into the room and read while your father sleeps." She kisses me on the cheek, giving my hand a reassuring squeeze with hers on the way by.

I turn and come face-to-face with the person I so desperately wish to hate because I know she's getting everything I've ever wanted in just a few short weeks. "Mind if we walk and talk? I've been sitting for awhile reading the sports highlights to my pops, I could use a little bit of exercise and fresh air."

"Not at all, a walk sounds perfect."

Perfect. Not exactly the word I would use to describe what's happening right now, but whatever. I gesture with my hand in the direction of the sidewalk, closing the front door behind me.

For the first ten minutes it's mostly silent, other than Emma mentioning how beautiful it is outside and how much she loves all the different trees this time of year.

"As fun as this is, and I really don't want to come off like a bitch, but why are you here?" The words fly out of my mouth before I have a chance to stop them.

She laughs, kind of obnoxiously actually, and if I didn't hate her so much, that laugh would definitely make me love her. "You are definitely bold Lennox. I think if this were a different life and we met under different circumstances you and I would actually be friends. But you are right for assuming I came here for more than just a leisurely walk on this beautiful August day. I came to invite you to the wedding."

My feet apparently forgot how to walk because I come to an abrupt stop in the middle of the sidewalk. "Excuse me?"

"Crazy right? I don't know, I just felt like it was the proper thing to do. You were such an important part of Graham's life and I truly feel like he would want you there, but I know him and he would never ask that of me. So I'm just skipping that awkward conversation and jumping into this one. Please don't feel like you have to come, but know that the invitation is there if you want it."

Okay, clearly Graham hasn't shared everything that happened between him and I with sweet Emma. Because if he had, I doubt she would be standing here with an open invitation to the biggest day of her life, instead she would be clawing my eyes out and telling me to stay the hell away from her man. At least that's what I would be doing.

Or maybe he has told her, and because she's such an amazing human inside and out, she still finds a way to rise to the top and be the bigger person. "I'm not coming to your wedding Emma." The words come out of my mouth more bitter and unkind than I plan on. "I mean, thank you, but I will have to gracefully decline. I hope your day is everything you have ever hoped it would be."

We turn and head back in the direction of the house, and as we get closer to the end she stops and looks at me. "I love him Lennox." Everything inside of me goes numb as I try to come up with the words to say back to her. "Great, me too", or "congratulations" doesn't really seem appropriate. "I don't know why but I feel as if something in him has changed since he ran back into you, and I can't put my finger on it. He says he loves me and that he can't wait to be my husband, but there is something he isn't saying. I don't know why I'm telling you all of this, I mean you are basically my enemy - "

I reach out and place my hand on her arm, "I'm not your enemy Emma. I know you love him, and I can tell he loves you too. Unfortunately for me, I also love him, but that's why I'm so okay with walking away. You're the best woman for him. You are whole, which is something I haven't been in awhile. Something happened to me a long time ago that broke my soul, I'm not really sure it can ever be fixed. Not even by Graham. You don't have to worry about me... my presence in this town is only temporary. Eventually I will only be a distant memory, and until then, I promise to stay away. Which includes staying away from your wedding."

Something in her eyes changes, at first it was almost like I saw fear, but now that's gone and in its place is sadness. "I'm sorry that my happiness comes with your pain."

"Don't be. Now don't you have a wedding to finish planning for? Stop wasting any of your thoughts or time on me."

She smiles, "Bye, Lennox."

"Bye, Emma."

"Tomorrow this will all be over sweetie." My mom kissed the top of my head on her way out of the kitchen.

Will tomorrow be like some magic switch that turns off the pain and heartache of knowing I will never be with the only man I've ever loved?

I doubt it. I really doubt it.

Chapter 17

Lennox

I wake up to the sound of a buzzing noise and quickly realize it's my phone vibrating on my nightstand. What the hell time is it? I reach over and see Graham's face lighting up my phone screen and hesitate before answering. It's two in the morning, on his wedding day, why is he calling me? Us talking is going to do nothing but complicate things, so I let it go to voicemail and set my phone back on the table.

I lay back and look out the window at the almost full moon lighting up the sky, and just as my eyes start to close my phone starts vibrating again.

Concerned that maybe this is something more serious than last minute cold feet, I press the green button to answer it.

"Hello?"

"L-lenny, heeeey." His words slur as he tries to get them out. "I miss you."

"Graham." I pause, is this how it's going to be for the next twenty years? Him calling me everytime he drinks too much and decides he misses me. "Why are you calling me? It's your wedding day."

"It shouldn't be though." His words sound more sober this time around.

"What?"

"Tell me not to do it Lenny, tell me that I'm making the biggest mistake of my life and we are supposed to be together. Damn it, just tell me you love me, sweet lips."

I sigh, "Graham, don't do this. You're only calling me because you're drunk and alone, just go to sleep and when you wake up in the morning, all of this will just be a foggy memory."

"God damn it, Lennox. I don't want you to be a foggy memory, I want you to be the person I wake up to every morning. I want to fall asleep every night knowing you will be the first thing I see when my eyes open. All you have to do is tell me you want that too and I will walk away, from her, from the wedding. Everything. Just say the damn words Len. Please." His broken voice cuts out as he finishes.

"I can't tell you those things. There is so much about me that you don't even know, and I promise you, if you did know, you wouldn't want me as much as you think you do right now. Emma is perfect, she can make you a whole person again Graham, you yourself told me that. Let her be that person."

His voice is quiet, and I can tell he is starting to drift off, "I love you so much it hurts Lennox Coleman. I've loved you for the last fifteen years and I will continue to love you until the day I die. I'm sorry I didn't fight for us back then."

His breathing gets louder and after a couple of minutes I can tell he has fallen asleep. I whisper "I love you too Graham," and hang up the phone. Setting it back on my bedside table. I'm not really sure what happens next, but I know I will definitely not be getting any more sleep tonight. Should I have just told him not to do it? Told him to walk away from her and run into the unknown with me?

I guess we will never know the greatness we could have had together, because in just a few short hours, Emma will be Mrs. Graham Thomas.

♡♡♡

"Lennox get up!" My moms scream from down the hall startles me enough to jump out of bed and hit the floor running. Jesus, what time is it? The last time I looked at the clock it was five in the morning.

When I get to my parents room my mom's upper body is laying over my dad's chest and she's sobbing, "Call 9-1-1. He's not breathing."

I freeze. "Mom you have to start CPR."

"I know Len, just call the ambulance."

Chapter 18

Graham

Last night, ugh, last night is a giant drunken blur starting with the shots on the party bus and ending with the strangest dream that involved Lenny talking me off the ledge of calling this whole wedding off.

"You doing okay baby brother?" Will's hand squeezes my shoulder as he hands me a tumbler with some amber liquid in it. My queasy stomach must come through loud and clear by my facial expressions because he continues, "Hair of the dog, just drink it."

I tip it back and choke it down, "Gross, what the hell was that?"

He laughs, "Thirty-year-old Scotch, according to our old man it's good luck on your wedding day. How are you feeling?"

"Man, I'm not sure whose brilliant idea it was to get plastered the night before your wedding, but it was a terrible mistake. All I want to do is crawl back into bed and wake back up when everything stops spinning. And to top it off, I had this crazy dream that I called Lenny and basically begged her to give me a reason to walk away."

"Let me see your phone."

Confused, I pull it out of my pocket and toss it over to him, "Why?"

He doesn't answer right away, "That wasn't a dream Graham." Turning the phone so I can see the recent calls. "Looks like you two talked for over twenty minutes shortly after I dropped you off at home."

Fuck. I was so convinced that it was just a dream I didn't even bother looking at my recent calls.

A knock on the door disrupts my mental rewind of everything we said to each other.

"I'll grab that. Pull your shit together, you look like you just saw a ghost."

"Hey, Will." The sweet voice of my soon-to-be wife should warm me but instead everything inside instantly feels cold. "I know it's bad luck for the two of us to see each other before the wedding and all but do you think I could have a few minutes alone with him before we get started?"

"Ahh… yeah. Sure. I will just be down the hall checking on the kids to make sure they aren't giving my mom too much grief."

I stand up and turn to find the woman I thought completed me standing in the doorway of my old bedroom in a beautiful mermaid style gown. Emma isn't overly curvey but you wouldn't be able to tell by the way this dress fits her so perfectly.

"Hey you." She smiles while closing the door to give us some privacy.

"You look beautiful Emma." I reach out and pull her into my arms, lightly kissing the top of her head, avoiding any disruption to her perfect hair.

She pulls back, looking me in the eyes, her light blue orbs looking a little darker today.

"Is everything okay?"

"I actually came here to ask you that exact same thing."

"Great minds think alike. Want to sit down?"

"No I better stand. I'm worried that once I sit down, I might not be able to stand back up."

An uneasy feeling settles in the pit of my stomach, something is off with her. And nothing is ever off with Emma Collins, she is always put together and ready for anything. "Talk to me Em, what's going on in you head?"

Her sad sigh gives it all away before her words even come out, "Are we making a mistake Graham?"

The words hit me like a ton of bricks. Although the same words have ran on repeat through my own head over and over, I never expected to hear them come out of her mouth. I stumble back, finding the desk behind me to lean against. "I...I don't know what to think anymore Emma. I know I love you."

"But you don't love me like you love her." It comes out more like a statement rather than a question. "You don't have to say it. I know. I can see it in your eyes, and hear it in your words. I honestly thought that I was okay with it, I thought we would get married and eventually your love for me would grow and mask what you felt for her. But as I was getting ready today it hit me, I don't want to settle for second best." She makes her way over to the bed and sits down, "Maybe I will sit after all. She's your person, Graham, anyone with working eyes can see that. I just wanted to ignore it and hope it eventually went away."

My words fail me, I want to tell her she's wrong and that we should get married because I love her so much that I can't imagine a life without her in it. But I can't. I can't because it's not the truth. The person that I struggle to exist without is Lenny. "I'm sorry Emma. Part of me wishes I would have never ran into Lennox again, then we would -"

She puts her hand up to stop me, "I read the letters you wrote her. I know it was wrong, but I was curious about what could be so important that you would keep it in an old shoebox after all these years. And that's where I discovered Lennox Coleman. The woman who really owns your heart and soul. I want that. I want to be loved so fiercely by someone that they write me a love letter everyday even though they know I will never read them. I want to be someone's first choice, not the consolation prize. She's a lucky girl to own your heart, and I pray that she will cherish it and take care of it the way it deserves to be handled. You are a good man Graham. Don't for one second think you aren't, and I know you hate the term but accept the fact that you ARE a hero and there was nothing you could have done to save Dean last year. It was just his time to go."

I cross the room and pull her into my arms, this time not caring that I could mess up her strategically placed hair. "I never deserved you, Emma Collins. You have always been way outta my league."

"You're wrong. But unfortunately I think I was just a Band-Aid that was sent to cover up your scars until you found your way back to the person who is meant to heal them. Let her in, tell her about Dean, she will be there for you because she loves you. I saw it in her eyes the day I met her, the torch she carries for you is still burning as strong, if not stronger than it was all those years ago."

I wipe the tears off of her cheeks and lean down to press one last kiss on her delicate lips. "What do we do now?"

"Well, now's the hard part. Now we get to go out there and tell all of our friends and family that even though we care deeply about each other, we've decided there won't be a wedding after all.

You may want to keep both eyes on my daddy. I know you have military training, but I am his baby girl ya know." She elbows me in the ribs as we open the door to go out and break the news to our family and friends.

Chapter 19

Graham

As I walk into my home the reality of what just happened sets in. Everything after we left the room flew by in a blur of crazy, from her parents yelling at me, to my parents asking me what the hell is going on and ending with my sister sitting there, holding Lauren with a stupid smug look on her face. She has been saying for months now that the spark between Lenny and I wasn't gone, and maybe if my stubborn ass would have just listened we could have called this whole thing off before it got this far. Emma could've stayed down in South Carolina and kept the job she loves, instead of moving all of her belongings up here to just turn around weeks later and move back.

I told her I would pack everything up and hire a shipping company to bring it all back down to her. But the idea that I will never see the woman I thought would be my wife by now again, blows my mind. We've spent the last three years together, and she was my rock through one of the hardest points in my life. But I didn't really think me asking if we could still be friends would go over well with the way her dad was murdering me with his eyes. I will call her in a couple months and check in on her.

But now the same question stands, what happens next? As much as I wanted to rush over to Lenny and kiss her until neither of us could breathe I knew I should probably take a step back and evaluate everything in my life. I know I want her, I've always wanted her, but the looming question of where we go from here scares the shit out of me. Her life is in New York, a city that is constantly crowded with people and loud noises and definitely not a place for someone who is struggling with PTSD.

I feel my phone vibrate in my suit pocket. Ugh, fucking Halee. "Sis, I'm not really in the mood for a lecture on how royally I've screwed up my life. I know, I should have listened to you and saved all of us the pain of today, but - "

"As much as I love to hear you say I was right, I am calling to tell you that Lenny's dad was taken by ambulance to the hospital today. JR just called and said the ambulance crew got him breathing, but he was in and out of consciousness the whole ride to Iron City Health. I'm not really sure what your game plan is for winning her back, but I would guess it should start by you being there for her."

"Thanks Hales." I hang up, grab my keys and run out the door without a second thought.

♡♡♡

When I arrive at the hospital, it takes a little more flirting with the front desk girl than I would like to admit. Because I'm not family and neither Lennox or her mom, Louise, are answering their phones, I'm supposed to have zero access to this area. But as I round the corner, and approach room 105 my heart begins to race with what I'm going to find.

The room is quiet, with the only sound being the heart rate machine beeping in the background. SportsCenter is playing on the TV, but it's muted and other than Russ Coleman lying perfectly still in the bed, the room is empty. I turn to find a nurse and ask where Lennox is but the sound of coughing brings my attention back to the once strong man lying in a bed across the room.

His eyes open as I make my way over towards him. Lennox told me he wasn't remembering her or her mom most days so I approach slowly to avoid causing him any panic.

"Graham Thomas," he coughs out. "You are a little over dressed to be in a hospital son. Save that suit for my funeral would ya?" I can hear the attempt of humor in his weak, hoarse voice.

Stunned, I stand there staring and wondering how the hell he remembers me after all these years. But when I fail to speak he continues, "Come sit down. We should talk. Stop standing there like you've seen a ghost." His words are frail but I do as he asks, taking the seat right next to the hospital bed.

"How are you feeling sir?"

Russ tries to laugh but it ends up coming out more like a cough, "Sir. All those years in the military really improved your manners, huh?"

"Yes, sir." I smile. "I suppose they did."

"You look good Graham, and thank you for your service. Louise and I tried to keep tabs on you through your parents. We are proud of you son."

My eyes glaze over as I try to hold back my emotions, while watching him struggle to find the energy to continue. "I'm fading Graham, and I need you to take care of my girl. She's strong and stubborn and Lord knows she will never admit to needing you or any other man, but don't let her push you away." He stops, his eyes moving to the window and then back to me. "Her and her momma tried to hide the rape from me because they thought it was best, but I knew. I knew it the moment I saw her face as she walked into the kitchen the next morning, with her hollowed out eyes and broken spirit. That boy broke her. And he's damned lucky that he no longer lives here or I would've killed him with my own two hands. Consequences be damned."

My heart starts to race and I can feel the sheer panic zip through me as I process his words, "Sir, I'm sorry but I don't know what - "

"Graham!?"

Her voice stops me mid-sentence. I look over and find a confused Lennox and Louise standing in the doorway looking back and forth between myself and Russ. "W-what's going on?" Mrs. Coleman's words stumble out as she makes her way over to her husband and sits on the bed next to him.

I stand up, my eyes never leaving Lenny's, and make my way toward her. As I get closer, her focus leaves mine and drifts back over to where her parents are. "C-can we talk out in the hallway?"

"Yeah, are you sure? I'm not sure what's going on but somehow he remembered me Len? You should go talk to him, it's crazy."

She smiles at her mom and dad, then her deep brown eyes find mine again. "It is crazy. It happened briefly a few hours ago too. The doctor said it isn't uncommon for Alzhiemer's patients to gain clarity at the end of their road. His body is shutting down, Graham. They're saying he only has a few more days at best before he's gone." She gives a weak smile. "Let's let them have this moment before he's gone again, and we can go talk in the hallway."

I follow her out of the room and for the first time notice she is still in her pajama shorts and an oversized sweatshirt with her hair piled on top of her head. After we sit in the chairs down the hall from her dad's room I ask, "Do you need me to go and get you anything? A change of clothes, coffee, food? You name it."

"Why are you here?"

Her words crash into my chest, of course she would wonder why I'm here. I was supposed to be married by now and halfway through my wedding reception. "Because I want to be here."

She sighs, "Graham." Her pause is long, "Why aren't you at your wedding?"

"Because there wasn't a wedding today Lenny."

"Shit." She stands up and starts pacing the floor in front of me. "Damn it Graham, you were supposed to marry her. She's perfect - "

Before she can spit out anymore nonsense, I stand up and close the distance between us, bringing my hands up to cup her face and our foreheads together. "You are perfect."

Her eyes close as she takes in a few deep breaths, processing the words I just said.

"I need you to stop worrying about me or Emma, or anything else besides what you need right now. You just said you only have days left with your dad, Lenny, what can I do? Do you want me here, or do you want to be alone with your parents?

Where's your sister, does she know? Do I need to get her a ticket and get her ass home?"

Her desperate lips find mine, and for a brief moment, where we are and what is happening around us drifts away. "I need you to not give up on me. I don't know how to handle all of this, and I do a really great job of pushing everyone away when I'm hurting. Don't let me do that to you this time, Graham. I need you, I've always needed you."

Her words hit me and bring me back to the conversation her father and I were just having. "Rape." I pull away only to find her pained expression, "Lennox who raped you? And when?"

She steps towards me, wrapping her arms around my torso, nuzzling her head into my chest. "Not now. I will tell you - " she stops and takes a deep breath. "I will tell you everything, but not today. My sister will be here in a few hours, and I just need the next few days with my family. But I promise, I will tell you."

I wrap my arms around her, holding her head with one of my hands as she continues to lose herself in my embrace. I place a reassuring gentle kiss on top of her head and try to reel in the anger that I feel building up inside of me. Someone touched her. They touched her without her permission, and even worse, Russ made it sound like it was someone from Iron City. "I'm here for you Lenny. I'm not leaving this time."

Chapter 20

Lennox

Death.

When you look it up in the dictionary it says, "*A permanent cessation of all vital functions: the end of life.*"

He's gone. The first man I ever loved, my hero, the guiding light in my life, is gone. They told us when we first got to the hospital that we would have a few days with him. But they were wrong. After asking Graham to leave, my mom and I spent a few hours in a room with the shell of my father. His brief moment of clarity lasted for about thirty minutes and then he drifted away again, at least in the mental state. That night my sister arrived and we all sat, reminiscing about the things he used to do and say until he took his last breath just before midnight. He didn't scream or cry out in pain as you would imagine someone would who was taking their last breath. No, he just slowly drifted out of this world and into the next.

The three of us sat there, holding onto each other, quietly sobbing as the doctor and nurses came in to unhook him from the monitors. And just like that, the world as the three of us knew it, was gone. Just like him.

Over the next few days my sister and I had to be strong when our momma was at her lowest. And while we all knew it was coming and that it was for the best, we all continue to struggle to adapt to this new life without him in it.

The funeral was a blur of emotions, along with the days that followed. And now I'm driving my baby sister to the airport so she can get on with her life and get back to being the careless free spirit that she has become.

"Are you sure you are okay here alone with momma?" We pull up to the drop off lane of the airport and she removes her seatbelt so she can face me better.

"Stacey, I will be fine. Momma will be fine. You just need to get back to that ranch and continue living. I will keep you posted on everything here." She really has been so much help these past few days. Having her baby girl home helped our mom in more ways than one.

"When do you have to go back to New York?"

"I'm not sure. I called them yesterday to let them know that pops passed and they told me to take as much time as I need. But I know I have to start thinking about heading that way. My life is there, but…" I pause. Stacey and I have been so caught up with everything around us that we haven't had much time to talk. If it didn't have anything to do with a funeral or taking care of momma, it was placed on the back burner until a later date.

"But?" She smiles her contagious megawatt smile. "Does a sexy soldier covered in tattoos and muscles have anything to do with your hesitation to go back?"

"Graham?"

She slaps my arm and looks at her watch, "Look, I don't have much time if I'm going to catch this flight but listen to me," she pauses. "You ready for this?" After I nod she continues, "I saw the way that gorgeous man looked at you at the funeral. It was the same intense way he looked at you all those years ago, like no one else was in the room. I used to dream when I was little that someday I would find a man who would look at me the way Graham Thomas looked at my big sister."

"It's not that easy Stacey."

"Nothing about the two of you has ever been easy, has it? This is your second chance Lenny. And I know you have secrets, I used to hear momma sob in the bathroom when she was taking a shower. I know something happened to you after high school. You don't have to open up to me but shit, open up to him. Let him back in. He called off his damn wedding for you."

"I actually think Emma called the wedding off - "

"Stop!" She yells. "Ugh, you are so frustrating and honestly for being one of the smartest people I know, you really can be an idiot sometimes. He loves you, you love him. Why are you making this way harder than it needs to be? Just dive in head first Lenny." She looks down at her watch again. "Really, I gotta go. And why the hell are you smiling at me like that?"

I lean across my car and pull my baby sister into my arms. "I just miss you. And love you so much. Thank you."

"I love you too, Lenny. Now go get your man." After kissing me on the cheek, she winks and grabs her carry on out of the back seat. "Bye Len."

"Bye. Fly safe."

I watch her walk through the sliding doors, blowing me one last kiss then disappearing into the airport, before I put the car in drive to head home. Everything inside of me wants to drive straight to Graham's and throw caution to the wind, but the reality of it is, I have a mom back at the house who needs me.

Everything else can wait.

Chapter 21

Graham

It's been a week since her dad's funeral and I've been trying my best to give Lennox the space she needs, but when her mom called me today I jumped at the sign that it's time to intervene.

The unknown local number that comes across my phone screen causes me to pause. These days you never know when you answer the phone if it's going to be a real person or a recording for a telemarketer. "Hello?"

"Hello, Graham? This is Louise Coleman, I hope it's okay that I got your phone number from your mother?"

"Of course, Mrs. Coleman, what's going on? Is everything okay?"

Her laugh on the other end of the line reminds me of Lenny's, "Mrs. Coleman. Graham I have known you half of your life, the majority of that time you've been in love with my daughter. I think it's about time you call me Louise, what do you think?"

This time it's my turn to laugh, there's no doubt in my mind that Lenny got her strength and 'to the point' honesty from this woman. "Yes ma'am, I think I can handle that."

"Ma'am." She sighs, "I suppose you are a work in progress. But I am calling you because if I'm being blunt, my daughter is just about on my last nerve. She is walking around here on eggshells and treating me like I'm a child. Please, for the love of God, come get her and make her do something fun. Would ya?"

"Yes ma'am, I mean Louise. I will be there in about thirty minutes, and Lousie..."

"Yes?"

"It's probably best that you don't mention me coming over to her, that way she doesn't have time to figure out a way to get out of this. See you soon."

So here I am, pulling up to the Coleman house, with something that feels like butterflies flapping around in my stomach. I don't know why I feel so nervous, it's not like this is the first time I've ever had a date with Lennox. But for some reason, today feels like the beginning of our possible forever. There's no expiration date looming over our heads, neither of us are engaged to be wed to someone else, the only obstacle I have is trying to convince her that Iron City is where she needs to be. But does that make me a selfish bastard to want her to leave her life in New York to move back to a town she hates? All I've thought about for the past few days is who the hell Russ was talking about. Maybe he wasn't one hundred percent accurate about the who part of it all, and maybe this happened while she was away in college. Not that it makes it any easier to swallow.

As I ring the doorbell, I force all of it to the back of my head knowing I'm going to have to be on my 'A' game if I have any chance of Lennox leaving with me today. She is so stubborn and if she thinks for one second that her mom needs her, it's going to be a fight to make her believe it's okay to leave for the night to clear her head and live a little.

"Come on in Graham, I believe Lennox is up in her room. Do you think you can remember how to get to it from the inside? I know you used to prefer coming in through the window back in the day." She gives me a knowing wink and I return her suggestion with a smile. I had a feeling she was on to us all those years ago.

"Up the stairs, down the hall, last door on the right?"

She slaps me on the shoulder, "You got it, sweetie. Oh and good luck. Lord knows you're going to need it with that one."

I take a deep breath and knock on the closed bedroom door. "It's open momma, come on in."

I open the door to find a half dressed Lennox, sprawled across her bed, typing something on her laptop. "Jesus, Graham." She jumps up and walks over to her dresser, throwing on the first pair of shorts she can find. "What the hell are you doing here?"

Peeling my focus away from her long tanned legs, I finally reply, "I'm here to kidnap you for the night. Pack a bag, we need to get on the road soon."

"Excuse me?"

"I chatted with your mom this morning and we agree that it's time for you to get out of the house for a bit. So I have a surprise for you. It's supposed to be a little chilly tonight and what I have planned for us involves being outside so maybe some jeans and a sweatshirt. But we are going to be gone all night so make sure you pack some pajamas." I pause, and take her in, with her arms crossed, hip popped out to one side and all of the sassiness that seems to pour out of her. "Or don't pack pj's, I'm perfectly okay with the option of sleeping nude if you are."

She walks back over to her bed and types a few things onto her laptop before I see her hit the send button and close it. "I can't go somewhere overnight, my mom - "

I close the distance between us and place a small kiss on the tip of her nose before saying, "Your mom is perfectly okay with you being gone for twenty-four hours. In fact, it might be good to give her a little space to breathe and figure out how to live in this house alone."

"Are you suggesting that I've been suffocating her?"

I let out a laugh, turn her in the direction of her closet where I can see a bag hanging on the door, "No ma'am, I'm suggesting that you pack a bag before I pack it for you and trust me to show you a good time tonight."

"Ugh." She dramatically stomps across the room, grabbing the bag and a few other things out of her closet. "I am going to need a few minutes, why don't you go chat with my momma. Since you two seem to be such good friends these days."

I smile and head in the direction of the door. "You got it, sweet lips. Trucks leaving in thirty minutes."

Chapter 22

Lennox

Can it be considered kidnapping when the person is thirty-years old? And who am I kidding? As much as I sit here, pretending like I don't want to be going on some romantic overnight getaway with the guy of my dreams, there isn't anywhere else I would rather be in this moment. Graham Thomas is the type of man most women dream about. When he walks into a room, his presence alone demands the attention of everyone around him.

Which is why when he walked into my bedroom a mere forty-five minutes ago, wearing his dark denim jeans, and plain grey T-shirt that's just tight enough to show off his washboard abs hiding beneath it, I was unable to tell this man no.

"Where are we going?" I finally break the comfortable silence we've been riding since we left my parents house.

He looks away from the road briefly and reaches his hand across the center column of the truck to grab mine. "Well it wouldn't be considered a surprise if I told you that, now would it?"

I kick off my sandals, bring my feet up to the dash and look back out the side window. "I hate surprise's." I mumble.

His laugh makes me smile as his hand squeezes mine before letting it go. "Some things never change sweet lips. Just relax and enjoy the ride."

'Whose truck is this?" I turn my head, glancing in the back seat.

"Mine. Whose else would it be?"

"Well, I don't know. I've only seen you drive your old truck since I've been back home. How many vehicles does one man need?"

"Baby, a man can never have too many trucks. But to answer your question, I have my 1980 Silverado, and then I have this one. I bought this when I was stationed down in Ft. Bragg about four years ago. And you're right, I do favor my old one most days, but for today's adventure we needed something better suited for the long haul."

I scoff again, frustrated that he won't just tell me where the heck we are going. "Why'd you cut your hair?"

His eyes narrow but never leave the road, "What is this the Spanish Inquisition?"

"I'm sorry. I was just trying to make conversation, we can listen to the radio or something if you want instead?"

I reach toward the dial to turn the volume up, but his hand gently grabs mine and he brings it over to meet his lips, placing a light kiss on my knuckles. "No, I'm sorry. Emma wanted me to get a haircut for the wedding and honestly, I felt so guilty over everything I was feeling about you, that I didn't fight her on it. But I didn't want to cut my damn hair. I've had this haircut for the past twelve years of my life and…" He stops. "I don't know, it's stupid but I kind of like the fact that I can grow my hair out, or not shave and it be on my own terms."

My heart swells at the idea of Graham the soldier not just that man who I feel like I know so well. "You wanna talk about it?"

He glances over at me, "Which part?"

"Any of it... the wedding, the Army, the Purple Heart."

"Well apparently the only people who didn't see the big picture of you and I being, in Halee's words, *soulmates,* was me and you. Emma came in and basically told me she couldn't play second best to you for the rest of our lives. And honestly, the weight that lifted off my shoulders in that moment was everything I needed to feel, and I knew she was right. I knew I still loved you Lenny, but I didn't want to hurt her. And you just kept telling me she was the right woman for me, so I had myself convinced that marrying her was what was supposed to happen. But I was so wrong."

My emotions get the best of me as my eyes begin to water, "How can you be so sure Graham?"

"Because this," he motions between the two of us, "right here, is the most right I've felt in years."

I take in a deep breath, trying to process everything he's saying. "And the Army? Don't think that my momma didn't talk you up when you were awarded the Purple Heart. You are a hero Graham."

"I'm no hero." His voice is stern and almost robotic, like he's said these words more times than he could count.

"Tell me about it. What happened to you over there?"

He sighs and runs the hand that's not gripping the steering wheel down his stubble covered jaw. "A lot, sweet lips. A lot happened. Let's just say I was too late. We were on a mission and I had this gut wrenching feeling that something was going to happen, I didn't know what but something. And then our tactical vehicle hit a roadside bomb and next thing I know I wake up to the sound of someone screaming next to me. My best friend, Dean, was lying there bleeding out alongside the Humvee, and I could tell by the smell of fuel and smoke that it was going to blow at any moment. So I ran over, pulled him a safe distance away and ran back to grab the other two men still inside. I got my men out just in time, barely avoiding the explosion, but by the time I got back to Dean, he was gone. I was too late."

My brain fails me as I try to find the right words to say. "It's not your fault Graham."

"Yeah, yeah. So they say. But it definitely didn't make seeing his wife and son for the first time afterwards any easier. Knowing that if I would have just stayed and tied his leg off to stop the bleeding instead of running back for the others, he would still be here today."

"He MIGHT be here today. You can't say for sure, and you saved two other lives."

"But I killed him."

"Graham Thomas, pull this truck over right now."

Startled by my tone he looks over at me before hitting his turn signal and pulls off at the next exit. Once we are safely parked in a truck stop, I lift the center console of his truck and climb over so I'm straddling his legs. "Look at me." His gaze continues to look around me and onto whatever is in front of the truck. "Damn it, Graham. Look. At. Me. This is not your fault, do you hear me. You did NOT kill him. Those terrible people over there that you spent more than a decade protecting us from, they killed him. You have to stop carrying the weight of this around with you and let it go. I know I didn't know Dean, but I can only imagine what he would say if he knew this was what you thought."

A smile breaches his face, "He would tell me to man the fuck up and let it go."

I reach my hand up, cupping his cheek and run the pad of my thumb along his lips. "Sounds like a plan to me, soldier."

Our lips meet for the first time since I left his house all those weeks ago, and it still feels like electricity zipping through my body and ending in my core. "You're pretty damn sexy when you take control and straddle me." His hands roam down my back, giving my butt a tight squeeze. "Thank you for the pep talk, I needed it."

"Anytime." I lean to climb off of him and slide back over to my seat but he grabs my hips, holding me firmly in place.

"Where do you think you're going?"

"Back to my seat, so we can get back to this surprise you have planned for us tonight."

"I thought you hated surprises?"

I crawl off of his lap, noticing the half chub that his pants are doing a terrible job at hiding and return to my side of the truck. "I guess I seem to be coming around to the idea. Let's go."

"Yes ma'am." He smiles and puts the console down that acts like a divider between our magnetic energy, before shifting the truck back in gear and directing us back towards the interstate.

Chapter 23

Lennox

"Um, Graham, did we just drive three hours to Detroit just to stay in this fancy hotel? Or is there more?" I glance around the parking lot.

"Lenny, you really are terrible at this whole surprise thing. Once we get checked in and to our room, I guess I can tell you what we are doing tonight."

We barely make it through the door of our suite before I'm throwing my bag on the floor and attempting to pin his massive body against the wall. He lets out a laugh and wraps his muscular arms around my shoulders, pulling me into a tight embrace. "Okay, okay. How do you feel about going to see a Matchbox Twenty concert tonight?"

I freeze and pull back so I can see his eyes, trying to gauge whether or not he is joking. Nope he looks serious to me. "Stop! Really?"

His unfairly handsome head moves up and down as the corner of his mouth lifts.

"But you hate Matchbox Twenty, and crowds. I asked you to go that summer after we graduated high school and you said you would rather eat dog poop than sit through a couple of hours of their terrible music?"

His chest shakes as he laughs, "Yeah, that sounds about like something I would've said back then. Let's just say I am a little more willing to endure a few things that I normally wouldn't if it means seeing a smile on your face like you have right now. And as far as the crowds go, the venue is outdoors and I got us lawn tickets. I will be fine, maybe on high alert, but fine."

I snake my arms around his waist, burying my head into his chest and inhaling the smell that is Graham. Woodsey but clean. "I don't know if I've ever loved you more than I do in this moment right now."

His body stills and I lean back slightly to gauge his facial expression. "Don't freak out, it's just a saying. It's no big deal."

"Say it again."

"Say what again?" Confused, wondering if he wants me to say "not to freak out" again?

"That you love me."

The look in his eyes is unlike anything I've ever seen in him. Worry almost. Like he needs some sort of confirmation of us. "Graham," I shake my head at all the alarms going off inside of it. "You know I've loved you for almost half of my life."

"Just say it sweet lips. Tell me you love me."

"I love y - " His lips slam into mine before I can even get the words completely out and before I know what's happening he lifts me, my legs wrap around his toned waist and he carries me in the direction of what I would assume is the bedroom of the suite.

As he gently lays me down on the bed, his eyes fiercely roam over my body like a lion assessing his next meal, before he kneels down and presses a firm kiss on my lips. "I've waited years to hear you say those words again to me Lenny."

His hand reaches behind his neck and pulls his shirt off, discarding it on the floor beside the bed. I take in everything he has to offer, this time knowing it's mine and not someone else's. But as he reaches down to unbutton my shorts, my whole body turns to stone at the realization of what could happen next. "G-Graham…" I close my eyes to try and control my breathing. "I can't do this."

Sweat starts to form around the base of my neck as my body fights with my brain to just let this happen. The bed dips next to me and swiftly Graham pulls me up into his arms in a tight embrace. "Len, just breathe. It's me. It's just me and you right now. We don't have to do anything."

I open my eyes to find worry etched across his beautiful face. "I'm sorry. I thought maybe that wasn't going to happen with you because, well because you are you. But apparently, even the amazing Graham Thomas can't chase away my demons."

"Who was it Lenny? Who did this to you?" His voice firm.

"Why don't we get around for tonight, and we can talk about this tomorrow?"

He shifts me off his lap and turns so we are facing each other. "Oh no, not this time. This has been running through my mind since that day at the hospital. Damn it, Lenny, please tell me what happened. Was it when you were in college? Your dad mentioned something about the guy not living in Iron City anymore, but I wondered if maybe he was just confused."

Am I ready for this? All the thoughts and memories that I've tried my best to hide from this man are about to unfold and what if he can't move past them? What if after he knows the truth about what happened the night of his going away party, he can't even look at me anymore because of the pain? What if all he sees me as is damaged goods, like I see myself? I suppose it's time to rip off this Band-Aid, but I'm terrified of what is hiding underneath it.

"I will tell you, but you have to promise me something."

"Anything." His concerned voice genuine and kind.

"You cannot for one second think that this is your fault, or that you could have done something to change that night. This is one hundred percent not on you, it's on me. And Jace."

His face morphs into shock as I begin to tell him the truth of what happened on August fifteenth, twelve years ago.

"Hey Jace, what are you doing wandering around out in the road. Get in, I'll take you back to Graham's." I point to the passenger seat as my boyfriend's best friend and partner in crime stumbles around the car and gets in. "What are you doing out here anyway, you're like a mile from the house?"

The words are jumbled as they come out of his mouth and all I catch is something about Graham leaving and thinking he knows everything about life.

I go to put my car in drive and his hand touches mine, "Please just drive around." His eyes are full of a sadness that I understand well. If he's anything like me, he probably feels like he is losing a piece of him tomorrow when Graham gets on that bus. These two have been inseparable since they were young, going through grade school together. If I had a dollar for every time I heard the phrase "ride or die" come out of one of their mouths, I could probably pay for my first semester at Columbia.

"How about we go over to the access and hang out for a little bit, let you sober up before I take you back? Sound good?"

He continues to look out the window and just nods his head once at my idea. Maybe I'm misreading his sadness for anger. But why would he be so angry at his best friend for wanting to go and defend his country? It's one of the most noble decisions in the world, which is the reason I decided to come to this party tonight and tell Graham that I want to fight for us. I want to make this work, anyway we can, because I'm not ready to let him go. Not now, maybe not ever.

When we pull into the access, he jumps out and starts pacing in front of the car, so I get out to join him and try to calm the storm that is brewing inside his head.

As I open the back door of the car to reach in and grab my jacket I feel him behind me, forcefully pushing my body with his into the back seat. Jace is big, not as big or as filled out as Graham, but enough that the weight of him on top of me is more than my small frame can fight.

But I try. When my brain realizes what he is doing to me, the warrior inside of me comes *out and I try. I scratch, hit, scream and bite to try and stop him, but he covers my mouth with one hand and uses the other to rip apart my leggings and underwear. After the fight in me wears down, I plead. Hoping that the Jace I've come to know and love is somewhere inside his drunken body, and will realize what he's doing and stop. But he doesn't.*

Within seconds he penetrates me and painfully thrusts over and over, his hand still covering my mouth while his other hand aggressively squeezes my breast. His muffled words come out angry and all I can make out is something about "Fuck Graham and his perfect life."

His body and thrusting slows just as the first tear trickles down my cheek and then he quickly pulls out, climbs back out of the car and slams the door behind him. Leaving me and my violated body and shattered soul inside of it.

At some point of my story, Graham got up and started pacing, but now he's sitting across the room up against the wall that his body slid down in defeat only moments ago. His eyes have the exact look I was worried about seeing. They are hollowed out, the only emotion left being pity. "Say something."

"I'm going to fucking kill him."

"He's gone." I start to stand up to go to him but I stop myself, deciding he needs a minute to process what I've just told him. "My mom said no one has seen him since that night, his dad resigned as undersheriff a few weeks later and his parents moved away too."

"I'll find him. Fuck Lennox, why didn't you tell me? I came to your house that next morning. Why didn't you tell me what happened?"

This time I actually get up and make my way over so I'm sitting directly in front of him. "Because this wasn't your cross to bear. I should have just brought him back to your house that night, I don't know what I was thinking. But he was so drunk and I figured he could use a friend, someone who knew exactly how he was feeling about losing you-"

"Stop." He lets out an exhausted breath and runs his hands down his face. "Don't make any excuses for that bastard. Lenny, this is not your fault either. Earlier you sat on my lap and forced me to recognize the different point of views, so I'm going to do the same for you. You were just being the kind person that I fell in love with. You saw the guy, who was supposed to be my best friend, in a moment of weakness and you tried to make it better. What he did to you…" He stops and it's obvious he's trying to control the emotions that are bursting to get out of him, "What he did to you, there's no excuse for it."

He shifts so he is on his knees in front of me, his hand cups my face and tilts it up so he can see my eyes. "This is not your fault Lennox. Okay?" I nod my head as he places a feathered kiss on top of my head. "Is this why you haven't slept with anyone else? Why that day when I asked you if I'm the last person who has made love to you, you said 'something like that?'"

I wrap my arms around myself, suddenly feeling vulnerable in front of the man who now knows most of my demons. "Yes. Any other time I've tried to take the next step with someone I all but black out, or scream. Who wants to deal with that kind of baggage?"

"I do." He pulls me into his arms again, "I want all of you, baggage and all. We can take this thing between us as slow as you need, sweet lips. I told you, I'm not going anywhere this time."

We lay there, wrapped up in each others arms, on the floor of this hotel suite for what seems like an hour. Eventually Graham breaks the silence, "We should probably start getting around for the concert. If you still want to go?"

I sit up and look at him through my emotionally drained eyes, "Oh, absolutely. Not even my demons can keep me away from a night with two of my favorite men." He lifts his eyebrows, obviously confused. "You - " I place a teasing kiss on his lips, " and Rob Thomas."

For the first time since we arrived at the hotel he lets out a boisterous laugh and helps me up to my feet. "Well by all means, we should get going." He slaps me on the butt and directs me towards the other room where we dropped our overnight bags. But before we walk through the door he stops me, "Is that it? No more secrets?"

I pause, knowing I should tell him about what happened three months after the night Jace raped me. But I can't. That's a secret that only I know, and I'm taking it to the grave. "Yes, that's it Graham cracker."

I lean forward on my toes and place a kiss on his perfect lips, knowing that if he ever found out what I did, he would never forgive me.

Chapter 24

Graham

I'm on sensory overload, between the loud music, all the drunk people and then Lennox. Free and careless Lennox, swaying her hips along to her favorite music in front of me. I'm actually surprised by the number of Matchbox Twenty songs I know, and a couple of times I've caught myself singing along to the words. I don't think my girl has noticed and if she has, she's not made it a thing.

I know we are nearing the end when the bands hit song, 3AM, starts. Lennox's hands fly into the air as she screams at the top of her lungs, "Yessssss!" She turns and jumps into my arms, bringing her mouth to my ear, "This is the song that I listened to on repeat, over and over, when I was in my dorm room at Columbia. This song is what got me through some of my darkest moments, and reminded me of the good I used to feel with you."

Before I can reply she turns her attention back to the stage and bellows out "It's three AM I must be lonely…"

Cautiously, I step over the blanket that is bundled at our feet and move up behind her so our bodies are flush and we are moving as one. I move her hair off of her right shoulder and slip my face into the crook of her neck, peppering kisses all the way up to her ear where I stop and whisper "Drops Of Jupiter".

Her body stills and she turns in my arms so we are once again facing each other. "What?" She shouts over the band and people singing around us.

I lean into her and repeat myself, "Drops Of Jupiter. That's the song I laid in my bunk and listened to over and over again, thinking of you. I hoped you were out there, somewhere, living your best life and all of your dreams were coming true. But I also hoped that you were thinking of me and missing me the same way I was missing you."

Her eyes are filled with emotion as she looks at me, almost like she can't believe the words that are coming out of my mouth. "Graham, I love you so much. And I hate that I didn't fight harder for us all those years ago. I hate knowing you were hurting just as badly as I was. Part of me wished you forgot about me the day you got on that bus, but now, knowing you longed for me in the same way I longed for you. I think it makes it worse. Why didn't we fight harder back then?"

"Because we were young and - " the song ends, and my shouting draws attention from the people around us. I soften my voice and continue, "Because we were young and didn't understand how magical and uncommon our love truly was. But now that we know, now that I know, you're not getting rid of me this time Lennox Coleman. I'm in this for the long haul."

She throws her arms around my neck. We slow dance and make out like the lustful teenagers we once were while Rob Thomas sings about timing and going home. With her in my arms, I have finally come to the conclusion that home isn't always a place, it can also be a person.

Lenny is my home.

Chapter 25

Lennox

This has been one of the hardest weeks of my life and somehow the man standing in front of me, struggling to figure out how to open the hotel room door, has brought so much joy to my day. Seeing Matchbox Twenty in concert has been on my bucket list for as long as I can remember and getting to experience it with Graham was the icing on top of the cake.

"He goes to war for our country folks, but he struggles to open a hotel room door." I giggle behind him.

Finally the green light flashes and it beeps, granting us access to our suite. He pushes open the door and waves me by with his arm. "I could get this door open a hell of a lot easier than using this stupid key card, but then I'm going to have to pay to replace it. Get your sassy butt inside, Coleman."

I drop down on the couch and take in the only man I've ever truly loved while he empties his pockets on the table, before making his way over to join me on the sofa. "I'm so sweaty and gross, I should probably take a shower before I get into bed."

"Yeah, that sounds good. I need one too but I will wait, you can go first."

I push the fear inside my head aside, "We could always save water and shower together?" Suddenly feeling shy.

"Uh, yeah, we could shower together. Are you sure you're up for that?" His stuttered words make his uncertainty of this situation very obvious. "I don't want you to feel pressured Lenny, I'm in this, we don't have to do anything you aren't ready for. We have the rest of our lives to make love."

I smile, suddenly feeling more daring. Kicking off my shoes before I stand, I slowly make my way toward the bathroom, shedding my clothes one-by-one until I'm left standing in front of the door with nothing but my thong and bra on. "Up to you soldier. I'll be in getting clean, feel free to come in and dirty me up a little."

After I close the door so it's only open a crack, I start up the shower and turn to look at myself in the mirror. Every part of me wants this, to be close and intimate with Graham, I just need to figure out how to let go of the ghosts of my past and allow myself to have it. I unclasp my bra, drop my panties and slip into the walk-in shower, closing the steam covered door behind me. And just as I start to lose hope that Graham isn't going to join me, I hear the bathroom door close and he slides into the shower.

He doesn't speak or even touch me, in fact the only reason I know he is there is because of the sharp exhale he released once he stepped in. "Lenny, I don't know if this is a good idea. Seeing you in here, naked and wet, I am a strong man, but this is really testing me."

I turn to find his eyes wandering up and down my body, and the only thing I can focus on is his massive erection. It was large years ago, but just like the rest of his body, I think it has doubled in size since the last time I've seen it. Instinctively, I start to reach out to touch him but pull my hand back when my brain catches up to what the rest of my body is thinking. "C-can I touch it?"

He laughs, breaking the awkwardness that momentarily took over. "You never have to ask for permission to touch it sweet lips. It's yours to touch whenever you want it."

My hand starts at his abs, slowly tracing the outline of each one while making my way down to the hard v's at his hips. And when my hand finally reaches his thickness, he lets out a breath that I didn't even realize he was holding. "God, Lenny. I've missed you, and this, so much." His words falter for a second before he continues, "Can I touch you?"

"Yeah, I think that would be okay."

His fingers start at my lips, tracing them with the precision I would expect from him, and slowly work their way down my neck, grazing over my collarbone. I appreciate his lack of attention to my breasts, assuming he is remembering the story I told him early and hoping he can forget it like I'm trying to. He leans forwards and places two delicate kisses on each of my nipples while slipping his hand lower toward my apex, running one finger between my folds.

I stop stroking him for a moment while I take in the sensation of being touched. This time knowing it's on my terms. "Just relax Lenny. It's just me and you right now. Let me make you feel good again."

Graham gently backs me up into the wall behind me, his skilled fingers continue to circle my over sensitive clit. Pulling my left leg up he rests it on the bench for better access, and brings his forehead down to mine so we are eye to eye. "Keep your eyes open sweet lips, just look at me." My body tenses as he slips one finger inside, slowly pulling it out and then entering two. "Shit Len, you are so tight."

I force my breathing to slow and I take deep breaths in and out, reminding myself this is Graham. His pace builds as he pumps his two fingers in and out of me while still rubbing my nub with his thumb. The unfamiliar feeling starts to tug in my stomach as I realize I am already so close to climaxing. "Graham - "

I squeeze my eyes shut as the sensations take over, "Open your eyes Lenny. Look at me." My eyes flash open and see the desire in his eyes just as the firework like explosions take over my body leaving me breathless and wanting more.

I feel warmth on my leg and look down to find his creamy white load on it, which causes me to giggle.

He backs up after placing a kiss on my lips and says, "Don't laugh at me. It's not my fault you are so sexy when you come apart, that you unmanned me right here all over your leg. That has never happened to me."

I lean forward, pulling him down to meet my lips. "I'm glad we can add that to the list of firsts we've had together then."

"Nope, we don't even need to talk about it."

"Oh believe me soldier, we are going to talk about this night for the rest of our lives."

He smiles, pulling me in for another kiss, "Oh yeah, why's that sweet lips?"

"Because, this is the night that everything changed."

Chapter 26

Graham

"Last night was fun." Lenny smiles over at me from the passenger side of the truck.

I pull my hand up to my heart, "Just fun, sweet lips? Apparently I didn't do a good enough job last night, if the only word that comes to mind is 'fun'."

She lets out an adorable giggle, the same one that won me over the first day I met her in gym class. "Trust me Graham, you definitely excelled at your mission last night. I honestly had no idea the amount of ways to experience an orgasm without actually having sex. I mean, that thing you did with your tongue, I'm not sure where you learned it, but I am forever grateful."

I reach my hand over and squeeze her hand, "Stick with me Lenny, I can show you a few things."

Something about her changes, and her head turns so she's looking out the side window. "Hey, Len. What just happened? Where did your head go just then?"

"It's stupid."

"It's obviously not stupid if it bothers you, just tell me."

She lets out a long exhale and then turns her body so she is facing me. "It's just... I don't know. When I let myself think about how many women you've probably been with over the past decade, I get all inside my head. I know that most people don't lose their virginity to their high school sweetheart and then have zero desire to sleep with another person for ten plus years. But it freaks me out to think about how you got so great at the things we did last night. I'm sure it came with lots of practice, with lots of women, and then I start to wonder why me?"

"Okay, take a deep breath and just relax. I'm not sure you even paused long enough to inhale or exhale during that entire rant." I glance over at her, but she's back to looking anywhere but me. "Hey, look at me. Don't make me pull this damn truck over when we are finally so close to home." She rolls her eyes but looks in my direction, "Good, now listen to me. Are you listening? Because I'm only going to say this once. You ready?"

"Jesus Graham, just spit it out already."

"It's always been you. Even when it wasn't you, it was still you. I don't know if that makes any sense or not but yes, have I had my fair share of meaningless hookups over the years? Unfortunately. But for a long time, it was my way of trying to move past you. Going out to those bars and picking up whoever was willing, was just how I filled my time. They aren't who I dreamed about once I was asleep, that was you. It's always been you. Okay?"

"Okay." A small smile graces her face, providing me with the view of her adorable dimple on her left cheek.

"Okay. Now that we've talked about how I was a massive man whore in the years we were apart, can we talk about one more thing before we put the topic to bed?"

"Or you could just put me to bed?" She gives a flirty wink that I swear has my dick already straining in my jeans at the idea.

"Jesus, Len." I rub my hand down my face and through the scruff that is starting to grow back on my chin. "As much as I want to do that, and trust me, I WANT to do that. Can we just talk about the whole Jace thing one more time?"

"Um… sure?" Flirty Lennox disappears and uncomfortable Lennox takes her place.

"Why didn't you tell anyone? You know, about what Jace did to you? I for sure know I would have heard about it if you guys reported it."

She uncomfortably shifts in her seat, "Ah, well, I guess I was scared. I mean it was Jace, and if anyone knows about all the crap he got away with because of his dad being the undersheriff, it's you. I figured it would just come down to his word against mine and why would anyone believe me if I was having trouble believing it myself?"

The anger that I've been trying so hard to push back surfaces. "But didn't you tell your mom? Why would she be so okay with just letting him get away with it."

"I told my momma about the rape, but it wasn't until a couple years later that I finally told her who it was. All she knew was that I was on my way to your house and I stopped to help someone who was stumbling in the road and that he forced himself on me, leaving directly after. I lied and said that I never saw the man's face who did it, and that it would do nothing but make things worse for me to have to relive it over and over if we went to the police. So she did what she thought was best for me, she cleaned me up and promised to keep it between her and I. I guess at some point she told my pops because obviously he knew enough to tell you. But he and I never spoke about it. I'm not exactly sure when he found out."

We pull into her driveway and I turn the truck off but don't get out. "You could have told me. I wish you would have let me inside that morning when I came to talk to you."

She places her gentle hand on my tense fist and smiles. "What would you have done? Beat him up or worse killed him?"

"Fuck yeah I would've. You were mine. You are mine, and he had no right to touch you or anyone else without their permission. I don't care how shitfaced he was, that's no excuse. God Len, it all makes so much more sense now. I never saw him again that night at the party, after I told him to go sleep it off. And I tried to reach out so many times while I was away at boot camp and after, but he never got back with me. I just chalked it up to him being busy with his new life, never did I fucking think he was avoiding me because he laid his hands on you. Fuck, Len! "

"I know. And trust me, the anger you are feeling right now, I've felt for a long time. But I eventually had to let it go, the only thing it was doing was suffocating me. I don't know where Jace is now, but I hope he lives with what he did to me for the rest of his life and I pray that he learned from it enough to never do it again. I told you yesterday, this wasn't your cross to bear. You were getting on that bus and leaving whether or not you knew, and I thought it was best you didn't."

I close my eyes to try and push away the tears of frustration that are on the brink of overflowing. Her calm voice pulls me out of the war zone inside my head, "Hey. Let's go inside and check on my momma and then maybe we can do something fun. It is Sunday after all."

That forces a laugh out of me, "Sounds good but what the heck does it being Sunday have to do with anything?"

She opens the truck door and hops out, "Sunday funday, duh."

♡♡♡

"Damn dude, you move on quick." JR slaps me on the shoulder as they load onto my pontoon. I thought today might be better spent just Lenny and I, curled up on the couch, possibly naked, watching movies all day. But when Halee called just after we stopped to check on Louise, seeing the way Lenny's face lit up, I knew we were going to spend our day surrounded by people.

Charlie slaps JR in the back of the head and quietly says something about keeping his damn mouth shut.

"JR, don't fuck with me today. I will kick you off of this boat just as quickly as you walked on." His words don't affect me, but I know what everyone thinks is something that Lennox is concerned about.

JR throws his arms up in surrender as he sets the overly obnoxious pink and white polka dot bag on the front seat of the boat. "That bag is really your color man. Is that where you keep your tampons?"

Charlie giggles as JR shoots daggers in my direction. I constantly wonder what is going on with the two of them. If he isn't working, he's spending the rest of his time with her and her son Tucker. You can tell he's crazy about her, but she doesn't really give much away on whether or not the feelings are reciprocated.

Halee, Luke, Quinn, Walker & Will all make their way down the hill from the house. And I glance over at Lenny trying to get a read on where her head is at. Once upon a time, these were all her people too, but that was a very long time ago, and she mentioned last night that being here, surrounded by everyone brings back a lot of things she has tried to let go of. I think she is referring to Jace, but I keep coming back to the idea that there is something more she's not telling me.

I squeeze her hand, "You good? If you changed your mind, we can always kick all of these people off of here and just have an us day."

She smiles, but I know her well enough to know that it isn't her normal smile. No this one is telling me that she is really trying to be okay, but isn't quite there yet. "No, I want to be here. I need to be here. I'm okay, I promise." She leans over and places her perfect 'kiss me' lips on mine. "Let's have a good day with our friends and then maybe we can do the whole movie and snuggle thing tonight?"

"Mmm…" I place my lips on her forehead. "Naked?"

That brings her playful giggle back, "That's a definite possibility Graham cracker. Definite possibility."

The loud sound of my brothers voice breaks us out of the Lenny and Graham bubble we were just encased in. "Why don't you two head back inside and work out whatever sexual frustration you have on each other? And the rest of us will go out and have a lake day."

My eyes never leave Lenny's now pink face. "No sexual frustration here brother. I believe that's you. How are things working out with Palmala Anderson?"

The guys laugh but the girls look between us like they don't get it. Finally JR clears it up, "You know PALMala, because the only action his dick has seen lately has come from Mrs. Right Hand."

213

"Ew. Gross." Halee dramatically exhales. "Can we just not talk about my brothers sex life, or I guess lack there of for the rest of today? Please."

I pull Lennox onto my lap, and snuggle my face into the side of her neck as I drive the boat out into the cove of the lake. Emotion surges through my body from my toes all the way up when I feel the way she completely relaxes as I pull her in close. So many things have crossed my mind since the day of my supposed to be wedding. Most of them being feelings of guilt for putting Emma through the ringer the way I did. But with Lenny sitting on my lap, breathing in the sweet vanilla smell of her shampoo, I know one thing for sure. This is exactly where we are supposed to be.

I bring my lips up to her ear and softly whisper, "I love you, sweet lips."

"I love you, too. So much."

Chapter 27

Lennox

Today is exactly what I didn't even know I needed. Sun, drinks, the perfect lake water, friends and Graham. Over the past few years I can say with one hundred percent honesty that I have made friends, but I also can say that I have without a doubt kept those people at arm's length. Dinners here and there, an occasional shopping trip or happy hour drinks, but I learned to not let people in. The more you let them in, the more they can hurt you.

But these past four hours reminded me of what it's like to have friends that are more like family. Because that's what all of these people are to each other, family. Once upon a time, I thought of most of them as *my people,* my group. In another lifetime, one where I didn't leave for Columbia, and Graham didn't leave for the Army, we could all still be out here, only Jace would be here too. In my head I believe that the stress of losing your best friend, along with the alcohol that night is what turned him into a monster. I have to think that the boy I knew would have never pushed himself on anyone unless he was so out of his head and so intoxicated that he had no idea what he was doing.

"Hey. Whatcha thinking about out here all alone?" Halee's voice pulls me out of the replay in my mind from all those years ago.

"Oh nothing, and everything. My mind is a mess these days."

She swims over and pulls her arms up on my raft so she is floating alongside me. "How are you holding up? I haven't seen you since the funeral."

"I'm okay. Honestly it's all kinda been a bit of a blur. My dad, finding out about the wedding being called off, then Graham whisking me away yesterday to see Matchbox Twenty."

"Wait! What? My brother, Mr. I-hate-Matchbox-Twenty-with-a-passion, took you to see them in concert?" She exclaims, and looks up toward Graham who is in a deep conversation with Will on the front of the boat. "Huh. Well if anyone would be able to get him there it would be you. Now skipping past the whole wedding thing, because I obviously have been saying that wasn't going to happen since you got back to town. Graham said he was able to talk with your dad a little and that he was fully aware of everything."

My body freezes at the idea of Graham telling anyone else about what happened. It's one thing that he knows, but it's completely different if the world knows. Then it's like it almost becomes real, and I don't want it to be real. I want to tuck it away in the little box inside of me and go on pretending like it didn't shatter the world around me.

"Ahhh… Lenny? Are you there? Were you able to talk to your dad at all while he was alert?"

"Um… yeah. When we first got to the hospital there was about a seven minute span where he was coherent and fully with us." I smile at the memory of what my dad said. "He told me loosen the reigns a little and not be so independant all the time. Which is so ironic because my entire life I was raised with this idea of being a strong, independent woman who could take care of herself. I still remember him saying to me "*Lennox Coleman doesn't need a man to complete her. She is the total package all on her own*". Yet his dying words are basically the opposite."

She lays her hand on mine. "Graham didn't speak much about what they talked about when he saw him…" Instant relief hits my body like a tidal wave. "…but he did say that your dad made him promise to look after you. As if anyone would have to tell my brother to keep an eye on you. It's pretty obvious he has two on you at all times."

I follow her gaze over to Graham who is smiling and looking our way. "I don't know what life has in store for us, Halee. My job is in New York, and he is here, far, far away from the big city. And he's made it so clear that he doesn't want to live in a place as crowded and hectic as New York. But what am I supposed to do? Walk away from my dream job?"

She smiles, "If it's for your dream man, you should do whatever it takes to make sure you are together." Halee looks back at the boat, but this time her sights aren't set on Graham, this time her lust filled eyes are fully focused on the man that swooped in and rocked her world. "Trust me Lenny, it's so worth it."

"Ron Smith offered to sell his practice to me." The words that I haven't spoken to a soul, not even my momma, come flying out like wild bees. Halee's head whips so quickly in my direction. "You know, Ron Smith, the attorney over on West Street?"

"What?! Yeah I know who Ron is, he does all the paperwork and contracts for my family's business. I didn't know he was retiring."

"Who's retiring?" Graham startles me as his raft floats up next to mine.

"Ron Smith." "No one" Halee and I reply at the same time. The difference in our answers cause her to raise one eyebrow at me in questioning.

"No shit? I didn't think that old bastard was ever going to give up the practice." Graham chuckles.

And before I have a chance to try and change the subject, Halee's big mouth blurts out, "Well apparently hell has frozen over, because he offered to sell his practice to big shot New York attorney here." Graham's eyes widen and Halee apparently takes that as her cue to leave. "I'm going to go make another drink, give you two some time to chat."

I watch her swim away after not only stirring the pot, but then putting the burner on as high as it goes. My eyes find Graham's and I can see the questions forming behind them.

"Are you thinking about it? You know, buying the practice. Staying in Iron City?" I wish I could tell him yes. Tell him I'm going to walk away from everything I've worked for and we are going to live happily-ever-after in this small town where my nightmares stem from.

"No. Yes. I don't know."

"Why didn't you tell me?" The pain in his eyes kills me.

"Because of this, right here. The look in your eyes when I tell you that I don't know if I can leave Simion and Clark, and I definitely don't know if I can come back here. I want you. I want you so badly it hurts, but what if this is all we were meant to have? A few months and then we have to get back to our separate lives that don't coexist well together - "

"Don't." He looks away from me and at the people only ten yards away carrying on conversations that won't alter their entire universe. "Damn it Len, don't you dare give up on us yet. We will make this work, we have to make this work." His last words drift out of his mouth almost like a silent plea.

I sure hope he's right because once again, we are running out of time. Only now, it's me leaving.

Chapter 28

Lennox

"Lenny sweetie, something was left on the doorstep for you."

My mom's words halt the email that I was in the middle of responding to. Everyone back in New York is hounding me about when I'm coming back, and as much as I'm trying to put it off a little longer, I know it's time. I've been home for just over four months. The partners at Simion and Clark have been more than generous with allowing me to take these months to be with my family and then properly grieve my dad. But it's time.

I click send, shut my laptop and head down to see what my mom is talking about. As I reach the bottom of the stairs, her face lights up like a christmas tree with excitement about what is waiting for me outside.

"What is it momma?"

"Will you just go outside and look? I'm not ruining the gesture of a sweet man." Ah. Graham. My mom always had a soft spot for Graham Thomas but it's even bigger these days. I swear he calls to check in on her more than he and I talk on the phone. And the other day I woke up to the sound of the lawn mower, only to find a very sexy, sweaty, shirtless veteran in our backyard.

It's sweet. He's sweet. From his patience to the topic of me leaving, to the restraint he shows when we are cuddling and messing around. We have continued to re-explore every base there is, but have yet to hit a home run. The panic that overtakes my body is something that neither of us wants to push and I know, as hard as it is on me, I can see it in his eyes. It's just as hard on him. He feels guilty about what Jace did. Like somehow it is his fault when we both know it's not. At least I know it's not his fault.

"Are you just going to stand there Lennox Louise or are you going to open that screen door and see what that handsome man left you? Geez." My momma scuffs as she walks out of the entryway and heads back towards the kitchen. I hear her mumble something as she goes on about romance being wasted on the young, which makes me roll my eyes. My pops was constantly surprising her with flowers for no reason, or spontaneous trips to the beach, because he knows she loves to read while listening to the children play and the waves crashing in off the lake.

Speaking of flowers, I open the door to find the cutest blue ceramic Ball Mason Jar, filled with daisies. My favorite - but what grabs my attention is the little envelope tucked into the stems of the flowers. I bend down to pick up the vase, smell the flowers on the way back into the house and after I set them on the kitchen counter I pull out the envelope.

"And he wrote you a note?" My mom continues to swoon from afar while unloading the dishwasher.

I look at her and roll my eyes. "I think I'll go read this in the backyard."

She smiles at me as I walk past her and out the back door to one of my forgotten happy places. The hammock. It's been years since I've laid in this, let's hope I can maneuver my way in just as gracefully as I used to be able to.

"Hey beautiful." I set my book down that we are reading in my English Lit class and glance in the direction of the walking wet dream that's heading my way. Graham is fresh out of the shower and so incredibly sexy in his light denim jeans, Iron City baseball shirt and bare feet.

He leans down and places the lightest kiss on my forehead once he reaches me. "Hey yourself. I didn't expect to see you tonight. How was practice?"

"Scoot." His hands gesture for me to move over in this already tiny hammock.

"I can just get out and we can go up on the deck. I don't think we are both going to fit in this thing, and even if we could, we would probably flip it before finding out."

"Just trust me Len, would ya? Scoot over, please."

I roll my eyes and hesitantly move to the left so he can weasel his way in. After a couple sketchy attempts and me trying to throw in the towel more than once, he settles down next to me. I giggle as he tosses Wuthering Heights onto the ground. "Two is a tight squeeze already, we definitely don't need the company or drama of Heathcliff or Catherine."

I look up at him in shock from where my head is resting on his chest. "Have you read Wuthering Heights?"

"Should I be offended that you are so shocked by this? I am more than just a pretty face ya know." I feel the smile on his face even without having seen it. Something about Graham Thomas radiates when he is truly happy. Before I can come up with an equally witty reply he continues, "I had that class last semester. And don't tell anyone, but I didn't really hate that book as much as I thought I would."

This time it's my turn to smile. "Don't worry Graham cracker, your secret love for old books is safe with me. Now you didn't answer me, how was practice?"

He lets out a groan, "Jace can't seem to get his shit together long enough to pitch decently. I have no idea what's going on with him lately, but his head definitely isn't in the game like it should be. And coach rode his ass hard- all the way to the bench. Told him if he didn't get his act together, he wouldn't be seeing the field from the pitching mound for the rest of the season."

I listen as I lazily draw out the words "I love you" on his defined stomach.

"I love you too, Lenny."

I giggle, "How is it you can tell a story with that much expression and still focus on what I'm writing on your stomach?"

"I'm always focused on you Len. In fact, I'm pretty sure my focus has been on you since the day you walked in with your ugly Matchbox Twenty T-shirt." I want to argue about his lack of good taste in music, but all I can think about is the sweetness in his words.

We lay like this as the sun starts to set, and my eyes roam the sky waiting for all the stars. "This is perfect."

"Mmmm..." is all that escapes him.

"Are you sleeping?" I lean up on one elbow so I can see his face.

"No, but how great would that be? Falling asleep with you in my arms, and being able to wake up to your crazy bedhead and morning breath every day?"

I playfully slap his chest, "I do not have morning breath."

"Everyone has morning breath Lenny."

"Not me." I smile and lay my head back down on him and point up into the now dark sky. "Look I can see the Big Dipper."

His arms snake tighter around me and if we weren't in my parents' backyard, or on this hammock, I would make my way on top of him. And as if my dad could sense my desire to do dirty things to my boyfriend, the back door slides open and he hollers, "Getting kind of late, why don't the two of you say your goodbyes."

I don't know if the tears in my eyes are from the memory of my dad, or if it's the reminder of just how simple things used to be for the two of us back then. School, baseball and soccer practice, sneaking kisses and affectionate touches when we didn't think we would get caught by our parents.

I opened the envelope to find an actual handwritten letter inside from him.

Sweet Lips,

I know this letter doesn't make up for the ones I destroyed from years ago, but I was kind of hoping it would be a start. Fifteen years ago you walked into my life and changed everything for me. I grew up watching my older brother bounce around from girl to girl in high school and that was one Thomas tradition I was more than happy to take over... until I met you.

It's crazy to admit, but I'm pretty sure I felt you that day before our eyes even met, almost like our souls instantly connected. I love you Lennox, I've loved you for almost half of my life, and I will continue to love you until I take my last breath. You are it for me... I asked you all those years ago not to give up on us, and this time I'm not asking, I'm telling you - we are not walking away from each other ever again.

Be ready at six tonight. I will pick you up. And before you throw a fit about hating surprises, just trust me. No need to dress up where we are going. Dress in whatever you feel most comfortable in, maybe just forgo the panties. Less I have to take off later anyways.

Love you so hard Lennox Coleman.

Always yours,
G

P.S. Even after all this time... you are still you, I am still me and we are still us. Forever in love.

I fold the letter back up, laying it down next to me and let the tears fall down my face. I have so many decisions to make about what happens next. But one thing is for sure, I am definitely not strong enough to walk away from this man. We have to figure it out. Together this time.

Chapter 29

Graham

Everything is ready.

I've spent the entire day preparing for tonight. And I suppose if I'm being real, I have been planning this night for about a week now. Every time I feel like we are close to having a break through between the two of us, something pulls her back. It's like I can see the spark in her eyes one minute and then the next minute they are back to looking almost as hollow as they looked that first day I saw her at Studio 365. I have tried not to push her on the idea of moving back here, even though I know it would make her momma so damn happy. But at the end of the day, she needs to come to terms with the idea on her own. If I just push and push, or guilt her into thinking she needs to because of her mom, she will just eventually resent the idea because she will feel like it wasn't hers to make. Out of the four languages that I speak, Lennox Coleman is probably the most fluent.

"Come on in Graham, Lenny is still upstairs getting ready. You look handsome tonight."

"Thank you Louise. How are you holding up?"

She smiles, and the dimple that she passed down to her daughter appears. "Just about the same as I was yesterday when you called. Just learning how to get along in this world without my best friend." Her eyes gloss over. "I'm just glad he is at peace. Watching him lose his mind the way he did tore me up. When we first found out about the Alzheimers he said 'I would rather die a slow painful death than lose my memories'."

I reach out and place my hand on her arm. My words failing me.

As I try to muster up something to say, I hear the wooden stairs creak and turn my attention to the woman descending them.

Breathless.

She's just wearing a simple pair of cut off jean shorts, and that same ugly Matchbox Twenty T-shirt from the first day I met her. But damn it, she looks perfect. All the memories and emotions I was

hoping tonight would bring back just hit me like a
747 and I have to try to remind myself to breathe.

I walk towards her and take her hand as she
steps down on the main floor off of the last step.
After I lay a light kiss on her temple I whisper, "You
look beautiful" in her ear. When I pull back to look
at her face, I notice the slight pink in her cheeks. I
love that after all these years, I still have the ability
to make her blush. "You ready to go?"

She just nods her head yes, and starts
walking towards her mom to kiss her on the cheek
and tell her not to wait up.

As we walk out the screen door, Louise
follows us out onto the porch, hand over her heart
and says, "You two have the best time. And do
everything I wouldn't do."

Lenny whips around so she's looking back
in the direction of the house, "Momma!"

Louise laughs as she starts to move back
inside. "You only live once Lenny."

I help Lenny up into the truck and I smile
when her eyes meet mine, "Well seems like I have
your mom's permission to fully take advantage of
your overly intoxicating body tonight."

"You never needed my momma's permission before." She arches her eyebrow, and I close the door, laughing as I make my way to the other side of the truck.

♡♡♡

"Why do I feel like I'm having déjà vu? You walking me down a hill with a blindfold on, it kinda seems like we've done this one other time in our lives." One of the things I love about her is her inability to just let go of the reins and hand over complete control. But I will give her credit, right now she is really trying.

"We are almost there, three more steps. Alright, perfect. Remove the blindfold."

She whips it off, messing up her effortlessly tousled hair in the process and gasps. "Graham. I love this. It looks just like that night all those years ago." Her hands are covering her mouth as she walks forward towards my old truck that is backed up, tailgate facing the lake.

"Yeah, only this time we don't have to worry about my creepy ass neighbor watching our every move. That was one of the things that drew me to this property, was there are woods on both sides. However, JR's house is almost directly across the cove over there, so I suppose he could be just as creepy if he owns a set of binoculars."

I walk up behind her and pull her body into mine, resting my head on top of hers. "We also don't have to worry about your mom kicking your butt for bringing all of the house pillows outside just to get laid." She looks up over her shoulder at me and winks.

I turn her around so our fronts are fully connected, "Who says these aren't her pillows?"

Lenny's eyes widen as she processes what I just said, and then we both bust out in a fit of laughter. "Just kidding sweet lips. I might have bought out all of the pillows at the Meijer in town for this occasion."

"What you didn't want to ruin your pillows?"

"Naw, I was just hoping that this could be a regular thing, so I figured I better just have a stash for nights we want to lay in the back of the truck and look at the stars."

She leans up on her toes and brings her lips to mine. Not like the gentle kiss she rewarded me with on the drive over here. No this one screams love with a little bit of lust and I can feel the want radiating off her body. I know because I feel that same desire and need inside of me.

We break away and I bring my forehead down to hers, silently willing her eyes to open so I can try and get a read on what is going through her mind. "Oh, Graham." Her voice breathy and unsure. "We have so much we still need to talk about, but can we just enjoy tonight? Let's just live in the moment and push aside all the adult things that need to be talked about for just one night. Tomorrow we can sit down and figure everything out, but tonight... I want you."

When her eyes finally open I can see the fear laced in them. Something is holding her back from jumping all into this with me and this feeling in my gut tells me it's more than just her job and friends back in New York. No, it's something bigger. Something she's not telling me. But instead of ruining everything I have planned, I push the little voice inside of me to the back of my head. "Sounds like a plan, sweet lips. Come over here and check out all the food, and let's make a drink."

Tomorrow we will face reality head on. But tonight, tonight is all about getting Lennox to let me back into her heart.

Chapter 30

Lennox

"So tell me about hot, older, more muscles Graham." He arches his eyebrow at my statement. "Oh come on, I feel like I know eighteen year old you like the back of my hand but this version - " I wave my hand up and down this toned, grey T-shirt covered torso, " - I don't feel like I know this version of you as well."

A smug, self-assured smile tugs at the corner of his lips. He pulls his beer up to his mouth to try and hide his amusement. "What do you want to know?"

"I don't know. Like... is your favorite movie still Top Gun?" I lightly draw my index finger on the tattoos that cover his entire left arm.

"Ohhh... Maverick. We should watch that movie soon. I don't think I've watched Top Gun in years. In fact, the last time might have been whenever you and I watched it in your parents basement. But if I remember correctly, I don't think I watched much of the movie that night. I'm pretty sure my face was between your legs- "

Heat zips though my body, ending in my core. "Yep." I stop him, all while trying to slow down my breathing.

Graham sets his beer down and rolls me onto my back, then props himself up on his elbow so his face is hovering just inches away from mine. "What Len? You don't like it when my mouth is on you? I didn't really think you minded the other night on my balcony."

His hand grips the back of my neck and pulls me in until our mouths meet. Then his fingers slip their way down my shoulders, giving brief attention to my boobs on the way by. But find their home down at my apex. He pulls the distressed edge of my shorts to one side where he finds my bare mound already wet and ready for him.

Judging by his pause and then deep inhale, I'm willing to bet he just realized I took his advice from his letter earlier and bypassed putting on underwear while getting dressed. "Lennox." My name comes out of him more like a growl then anything.

"I want you, Graham. All of you this time."

His hesitant but hopeful eyes flash open, "Are you sure? Don't feel like we have to do anything just because of this whole stupid truck thing."

I smile, "This is not stupid. This is the second sweetest thing anyone has ever done for me."

"Oh yeah? And what was the first thing?" He pulls back, trying to get a read on whose ass he needs to kick for one-upping him.

"The first time you did this for me." I swallow, trying to find the right words. "I remember being so nervous that night because my body wanted you, no, craved you so badly. But I was all inside my own head and worried that everything would change after we had sex for the first time. And I was right, everything did change. I felt a closeness with you after that night that has stuck with me all these years. I feel that same uneasiness tonight that I did all those years ago now, so just be gentle with me."

And just like that, all the worry that was recently taking up space in his mind disappears and he smiles at me while unbuttoning my shorts with his hand that moments ago was cupping my core. "Trust me sweet lips, I'll be gentle. At least the first time." He winks and I feel my insides churn with the anticipation of knowing there will be more to come after the first time.

He pulls my shorts down my legs and just like all those years ago, throws them over the side of the truck for us to find later. Then pulls me forward into the sitting position so he can remove my top, leaving me sitting in just my lacy blue bra. Graham leans forward and reaches around to unclasp it but I grab his hand before he gets there. "I think maybe it's your turn to shed some clothes there soldier. You seem a little overdressed compared to me."

That smile, the one that would melt my panties, if I were wearing any, appears again as he reaches behind his neck and pulls at the collar of his shirt to remove it in one swift motion. "Yes ma'am," he says as he discards it in the pile of clothes we've now started on the lawn.

Within seconds this dreamboat of a man is butt naked in all of his glory kneeling in front of me, while giving the "your turn" eyes. I reach my arms behind my back, unclasping the last piece of fabric holding us back from being completely bare to each other. And we both exhale deeply as our eyes meet.

"Are you sure about this Lenny? Because it might physically kill me but we can stop." I laugh at his words because I feel like he said the same thing to me the first time we were about to make love in the back of this pick up truck.

"I've never been more sure of anything in my life."

And that's all it takes. Those words release the caged up man that I've been basically sexually teasing for the past few weeks. Shit probably even months since he told me that he and Emma never had sex again after he ran into me that day at the salon.

The scratchiness of the stubble on his chin pulls me out of the rabbit hole I was quickly going down, and I lose all sense of control when his mouth reaches my throbbing core. "Oh, God!" I scream out as his tongue circles my clit and he slowly slides one and then two fingers inside of me.

All it takes is a few strokes of his tongue and him slightly curving his fingers upward towards the sweet spot inside of me that sets my insides off like a grenade. My legs and stomach tighten, while my hands roam their way over my breasts and down to his hair that's finally starting to grow back again. "Graham, I'm - " And before I can get the words out, my body is falling over the edge, fully consumed by the wave of heat taking it over.

I start to come down but his relentless mouth doesn't let up, while his fingers begin in a circular motion inside of me. Part of me wants to tell him to stop, because the sensation of it all is too much. But everything is lost when the second orgasm shakes my body like a tsunami, taking me to places I've never even known were possible.

This time when my body relaxes he looks up, bright blue eyes hooded with desire for more, and places one small kiss on my mound before crawling his way up my body.

"That. Was. Incredible." I say in between breaths.

He laughs and kisses me on the nose as he lines his shaft up to my entrance. "Are you sure about this?" Worry stretched across his face one last time before I nod my head, giving him the silent reassurance he needed before entering me. "Keep your eyes open Lenny. It's just me and you here. If at any point this becomes too much, just tell me to stop and I will.

I nod again, biting my lip while staring into his eyes he slowly slides the tip of himself into me. "Wait!" His body freezes, but he doesn't pull out. "Condom. I'm not on birth control."

Graham lets out a sigh as he lowers his head to my chest and places a tender kiss just below my collarbone. "Condom, right." He pulls back out of me and I'm amazed at how empty my body feels without his fullness inside of me.

I close my eyes and take a deep breath, willing my brain to be okay with what is about to happen. I need this to be okay. We need this. The truck bed dips slightly as he climbs back up, his massive erection covered this time. And after resuming the position he was just in, Graham's eyes lock back on mine and he asks the same question as before. "You still sure?"

I giggle, "Just get inside of me already, would ya?" And within seconds I am feeling the fullness of his cock inside of me, causing all the alarms to go off in my head.

Graham must sense something is wrong because he stops, "Lenny, open your eyes. It's just me. It will always just be me. I promise you that."

My body relaxes and he slowly starts to thrust in and out of me, the friction of his skin on my already sensitive nub causes the sensations in my body to start to build again. "Faster." It comes out more like a breath, but he hears me and starts to pick up speed. His right hand roams down my side, grabbing my thigh and bringing it up so he can penetrate deeper.

"Baby. This. Is. So. Good." He says in between thrusts. But I can't seem to get the agreeing words that are on the tip of my tongue out because I am once again on the brink of my own release.

"Graham, I'm so close."

I feel his shaft tighten from inside of me and the rest of his body tense up as I begin my free fall into my third orgasm.

We both just lay there, wrapped up in each other, his fullness still inside of me as we try to calm our erotic breathing. Moments later he pulls out, removes the condom and chucks it to the opposite side of the truck that our clothes are on.

"You okay?" He asks as he lays down and gently tugs my body over to his so I'm curled up into his side.

"Mmmmhmmm." It's the only thing my brain seems capable of giving him.

His fingers lift my chin so we are face-to-face, our noses just millimeters apart. "Talk to me Lenny. Are you okay?"

I know his question has a lot of meaning behind it. But I refuse to allow Jace to take this moment from us. "I am so okay Graham cracker. In fact, this might be the most okay I've been in a really long time. Thank you."

I tuck my head back into the crook of his shoulder as his torso begins to shake from laughter. "Len, did you just thank me for sex?"

"No. Well yes. That was amazing. But it's more. Thank you for being just as patient with me now as you were back then. Thank you for doing this tonight. It sounds so crazy but right now all I can think about is how grateful I am that you walked into the hair salon that day. Because I'm not lying when I tell you, it's been twelve years since I've felt as whole as I do right now. And that has everything to do with you. So thank you."

His lips place a gentle kiss on top of my head. "Anytime sweet lips. Anytime."

Chapter 31

Lennox

The chilly September breeze coming in off the lake through the open slider wakes me out of the dream I was having. A dream. Not a nightmare. Lately the nightmares that used to plague my nights are few and far between. I think I have the beautiful man laying next to me to thank for that. He came in one day and started to chase all my demons away.

I look over to find a similar view of what I woke up to all those months ago after the night out for my birthday. But this time it's a naked Graham laying on his stomach, white bedsheet low enough to show off the dimples on his lower back. His arm with the tribal tattoo again draped over my middle. The only difference this time is, this man is mine. In every sense of the word. He doesn't have a fiancé in another state.

"I love your bedhead in the morning." His raspy bedroom voice pulls me out of my daze. "What are you thinking so deeply about? All those toe curling orgasms I gave you last night?"

I smile and look over at his crazy blue eyes that are somehow even more blue in the morning. "You don't have any other fiancés I need to worry about, right?"

He flings the covers back and pulls me into his arms as he tickles. "Nope, not unless you want to take on that title?"

My body freezes. It's not as if I haven't dreamt about being Mrs. Graham Thomas since I was about seventeen-years-old, but we still have so many things to work through before we even think about getting married.

"Relax, Len. It was a joke. I mean kinda. I plan on marrying you, and having babies with you…" He peppers kisses along my neck, and I should be swooning at the idea of what he's saying but I can't. "I can't wait to build a life with you Lennox Coleman. Have you thought anymore about staying in Iron City?"

I roll out of his arms to my side and prop my head up on my hand. "Why don't we get around, maybe make some breakfast and then we can talk about things?"

He lightly pinches my nipple that's hanging out the top of the sheet I just pulled up over myself. "Yeah. Breakfast, then talking." He spanks me on the butt on the way out of the room.

♡♡♡

"Damn, sweet lips. If I'd known you could cook an omelet like this, I would have chased your fine ass down years ago." His light hearted smile melts my panicked heart a little. There is so much he doesn't know and in order for us to take this relationship any further he needs to know the truth, and understand why I did what I did.

"One of the many things my dad taught me over the years. He always claimed that a way to a man's heart was through his stomach. However, I'm not really sure how my momma snagged him when she could barely boil noodles when they met."

I slide my plate forward a little, and Graham notices that I've barely eaten any of my ham and cheese omelet. "Are you not hungry?"

"No. I guess I'm not much of a breakfast eater."

"Ahhh… so breakfast was just your way of getting out of having a serious conversation earlier. Out with it Coleman. What's eating you up? Is it leaving New York?"

"Yes and no. I've thought a lot about that and honestly I think I would love having my own practice here in town. It was always my dream when we were in high school. You know, go to New York, attend Columbia, and then move back here and start my own practice." I shift in my seat, picking up my fork to shift the food on my plate around for the tenth time.

"Okaaay? So what's wrong? Is it Jace?" The sound of his name instantly halts my breathing. "Because I have been meaning to tell you that I called up one of my buddies that I used to serve with, he's a private investigator, I asked him to find out where that bastard is."

Suddenly my other problems drift to the back of the line. "Why?" My gaze meets his determined eyes, and for the first time ever, I find myself face-to-face with Sergeant First Class Thomas, not the Graham Thomas I know and love.

"Because Len, that mother fucker touched you. He was my best friend and he laid his hands on you and took something you weren't offering. Fuck, even if you were offering it to him, it's his job as my best friend to say no. He didn't just cross a line, he erased the damn thing. He has to pay for what he did." He stands up, walks across the room to the kitchen counter and places his hands down, allowing his head to fall between his shoulders.

"And you don't think I should have a say in this? You didn't think about asking me if I thought he needed to be found? You're right Graham, he did cross a line. But you are looking at this selfishly. You are looking at how it has affected you since you found out. Well how about me, and how I've had to live with it everyday for twelve years? I don't want to find him. I don't ever want to see his face again, ever."

"Damn it, Len. You didn't have to go through that alone, you chose not to tell me what happened. You chose to shut me out and who says you have to see him? I'm not going to send him a letter that says "you have been cordially invited back to the place where you raped - ""

"STOP!" I take a deep breath and try to find the control I worked so hard to achieve over the years. "Just stop. I've told you, this isn't your cross to carry. What are you going to do, find him and kill him?"

"I can't say that the thought hasn't crossed my mind a couple times. But no, Lenny, I'm not going to kill him. I don't even know if I would go to wherever Jace is now. I just want to know that he is nowhere near you. I need to know. Can't you understand that?"

He walks toward me but I take a step back, which runs me into the back of his sectional couch. I crave his touch but I also need my space right now. Space to sort out everything that is rapidly firing off inside my head.

"Lenny, I just want to know you're safe. And someday when we have kids, I want to know that sick mother fucker is nowhere near my family." His eyes plead to let him come closer but the words he just said rip through me like a semi. He wants kids.

"Graham, I don't want kids."

"What?" Confusion hits. I know I need to tell him everything. It's now or never, and I already lied to him that day of the Matchbox Twenty concert when he looked me in the eyes and asked me if I told him everything. Because I didn't.

"You might want to sit down for this next part."

"I'm fine."

I take a deep breath and try to find the courage I need to go back down this dark road I've avoided for so long. The road I traveled alone because I couldn't even bring myself to tell my momma about what I did.

"I was pregnant Graham.

He stumbles backwards until he hits the counter. I want for him to say something, anything, but instead he just stares at me like he can't believe the words that came out of my mouth.

After moments of nothing, I continue. "I was at Columbia already when I found out. I thought it was just homesickness or anxiety from what happened that night, so when I kept getting sick I ignored it and hoped it would go away. But after I missed another period I decided I should probably check to make sure. So at eighteen-years-old, I got on the bus and traveled downtown to the closest drugstore and bought a pack of two pregnancy tests." I laugh. "I was so nervous about other people seeing what I bought, as if any of them knew me or even cared that I could be knocked up at eighteen. But I still shoved it into my jacket, out of sight until I was safely back in the girls' dorm room bathrooms on campus."

I look back at Graham but I can't seem to get a read on what he's thinking. "I thought the first one had to be a mistake so I waited about an hour before I took the second one. But when I saw that the second test was positive too, the panic really started to set in. What was I going to do? Here I was, at the school of my dreams on a full ride scholarship and I was what, going to throw it away on a baby that could be half of the man who raped me? I was going to have to look into this little baby's eyes for the rest of its life and love it even though I hated the way it was conceived?"

His hands rub up and down his face before he stills, and I hope he has forgotten the event that happened the week before he left for basic training. "The broken condom." He pales when his eyes find mine again. "We broke a condom the week before I left, and you weren't on birth control."

I watch as his brain connects the dots of the reality I've had to live with since I walked out of that clinic all those years ago. "Graham…"

"Lennox, that could've been my baby!" He shouts as he starts pacing again. "That could have been *our* baby Lenny. How could you - "

"Don't! Don't you dare judge me. Do you think for one second I don't tourture myself with the idea that we could have a twelve-year-old right now. But what if it wasn't yours? There was a fifty-fifty chance the baby wasn't yours. And honestly even if it was, what were we going to do Graham? At that point you were finishing up basic and starting your career in the Army, and everything I had ever worked for was happening. We weren't ready to be parents. We were still kids in so many ways ourselves."

His body is tense as he looks out the windows that overlook the lake. "That wasn't your choice to make."

"But it was. It was one hundred percent my choice to make and I made it. I did it all by myself. I walked into that clinic that day and took this medicine that resulted in so much cramping and blood. I needed someone, anyone, and yet I did it on my own, too afraid of what the outside world would think of me if they knew. You think this is hard for you? Try being in my shoes. Try having a boy who you grew to think of as your brother, strip you down and take everything from you. And just when you start to think you can actually move past that and start a new life in a new city you find out you're pregnant, and there's a good chance it's his. Not the child of the man you were in love with. It wasn't easy Graham. Nothing about my life after that night was easy ever again, but I've dealt with it the best way I could."

I walk towards him, hoping that if our bodies can just touch it will soften the exterior and he will let me back in. He turns around when the floor creaks behind him, his eyes stone grey. No longer the man I was just laying beside this morning. "I think you need to leave." His words startle me, and I open my mouth to speak but he beats me to it, "Please Lennox. Just leave."

So I do. I walk over to the door, grab my purse off the table and leave. "Bye, Graham" I whisper as I shut the door. Knowing this was the goodbye that I saw coming all along.

Chapter 32

Graham

"Will, open the door asshole, I know you're in there." I feel slightly bad about pounding on my brother's door at this hour of the night, but I know it's his weekend without the kids so I guess it makes this a little better. At least it's just his ass I'm waking and not my niece and nephew.

Finally the door opens, and there stands my big brother, butt ass naked holding his junk in his hand that's not propping him up on the wooden door. "This better be fucking important Graham."

"I could've been a dad."

His face sobers and he waves me into the house. "Go grab a beer. Let me throw some clothes on and ask my *friend* to leave."

Ten minutes later Will comes out of his bedroom with a girl that looks like she's barely old enough to drink let alone old enough for him to be fucking. After walking her out like the gentleman he likes to pretend to be, he stops at the fridge for a beer and plops down on the couch across from me.

I don't even know where to start with him, so instead I just raise my eyebrows and give him a "What the fuck are you doing with your life bro?" look.

"Fuck you, Graham." He throws a pillow at me that I assume his soon to be ex-wife picked out. "Don't show up at my house at eleven o'clock at night spewing some bullshit about being a father and then judge me for having a woman here."

"Woman?!" I laugh, "that girl was a child, did you at least ID her before taking her to the bedroom? Jesus. You might not have to worry about her husband coming after you, but I'd watch out for her daddy."

He takes another long pull from his beer and looks me square in the eyes. "Why are you here Graham? I'm horny as shit and apparently not getting laid tonight and my patience with you is wearing really thin. Talk."

I look around the room, trying to find anything to focus on besides my brother's eyes. I know he will read all of my emotions with one look.

When I don't say anything he speaks up. "Is Emma pregnant?"

I jerk my head in his direction. "What? No! It's not Emma."

"Okay so Lennox? Unless you're boning someone else in this godforsaken town that I don't know about."

I exhale and run my hands through my hair, placing them on my neck. "She was pregnant. Twelve years ago."

Will's eyes widen as he does the math and everything clicks into place in his head. "No shit? What happened to the baby?"

"She had an…" I can't even bring myself to say the word. In my family we were brought up to believe abortion isn't an option. If you're old enough to be fooling around, you are old enough to handle the responsibility of having a baby. And all day I sat in the back of my truck that's still parked down by the lake, laying on the pillows and blankets Lenny and I made love on top of, and I tried to understand why she didn't come to me. Why she thought this was a decision she had to make on her own. "…abortion."

"Damn." My brother's hand rubs the scruff on his chin that is basically identical to mine while he stares at me. Probably trying to figure out what to say, and how to fix this. Just like I've been doing all damn day. "And you had no idea? Back then I mean?"

"Not a clue." I find myself suddenly needing to defend Lennox and the actions she took. "But seriously Will, there is so much you don't even know. Things that I just found out about recently."

I sit back, knowing that by telling him I am breaking Lenny's trust, but at the same time I know I need to talk this out with someone. And why should it not be Will, he is one of the best men I know, if anyone will help me understand what happens next with Lennox and I, it's him. "I'm going to tell you something, but it can't leave this room Will. Ever. Got it?"

♡♡♡

"That weasley motherfucker. I thought it was so weird how he just up and disappeared and then not long after his dad resigned and they moved away. Our families were so close, and mom and dad said they never heard from them again once they were gone." Will has been pacing back and forth behind the couch since about five minutes into me explaining everything. If he doesn't stop soon, I'm pretty sure he is going to put wear spots in his beautiful oak floor. "Please tell me you know where he is?"

"Well, that's kinda what started this whole fight today. I told Lennox that I got ahold of an old Army buddy and that he's putting feelers out to try and find Jace's location. But she lost it, basically saying it's not my place and she doesn't care where he is."

He rubs his hand down his face and walks over to the fridge to grab another beer. "You want one?"

"Naw, I'm good. Thanks though."

"I can't say that she's wrong. I understand your need to find him, but you also should've ran that by her before you just went ahead and did it. And as far as the abortion goes, you have to try and see all of this through her eyes. She was alone at Columbia, scared and broken, not just from losing you but also from what he did to her. I get it. I know you don't like it, but you have to get it. And even if you don't, you have to accept that she's right. It was one hundred percent her decision to make."

I sigh, knowing his words are the same ones that have been playing in my head since she said them this morning. "I don't think I'm upset at her Will. Honestly. I think I'm pissed off that she was on her way to our house that night to be with me. To tell me that she would make this work between us, and he screwed that up. And then if that isn't enough to wrap my head around, I find out she had a baby growing inside of her, a baby that could have been mine and out of fear that it was his, she made it disappear. That's two things he took from me. First Lennox and then the possibility of being a father. But I'm supposed to sit here on my hands and not track this fucker down?"

He walks over and sets his hand on my shoulder, the same way he used to when I was younger. "I get it. You want my advice?" I look up at him. "Go home, sleep on it, and when you wake up in the morning, hopefully everything will be a lot more clear."

"Yeah. Hopefully."

Chapter 33

Lennox

I pick up the final article of clothing lying on my bed and place it in the suitcase before I zip it up. I needed to be back here, in Iron City, these past few months. The time spent with my pops and momma is irreplaceable, but it's also time for me to head back to my life waiting for me in the city. My life where I can walk into the local deli to grab a sandwich and I don't have to listen to the table of older woman in the corner gossiping about how I broke up the marriage of Graham and that *sweet southern girl Emma.* My life where there isn't a memory of Graham and I waiting behind every corner. I may be leaving my heart here, but I need to move on with my life in New York. I called Ron Smith first thing this morning to thank him for trusting me to take over his practice, but that right now, I needed to head back home. He let out his infamous chuckle and said, "Well it will be here waiting when you get back." Like he knows something I don't.

Sadly, other than to visit momma, I won't be coming back here. And hopefully, I can talk her into coming to the city for holidays, less memories of dad there. Less memories of everything there.

"Are you sure I can't convince you to stay Lenny?" I turn and look at my momma. Fifty-six-years old and she looks like she's still in her early forties. It's sad to admit but I think after losing dad, some of the stress and worry lines disappeared. "I think you should at least go over and talk to him sweetie. I'm sure it was a lot for him to take in."

What she isn't saying is that it was a lot for her to take in. When I came barging through the door yesterday morning with tear stained cheeks there was no way I was getting around telling her what really happened to me all those years ago. What broke me more than the actual rape itself.

"Oh, Lennox. Sweetie, I wish you would have told me." The same pain that was written all over Graham's face is now stretched across my moms.

"What would you have done? I was in no condition to be a parent. Especially not to a child that could have been his." I never told her because I didn't want to see the look she's giving

me right now. It's not quite disappointment but it's something. And whatever it is, it doesn't sit well with me. "I'm sorry momma."

The sobs I've been holding back finally escape and my mom jumps up from the kitchen bar stool to pull me into her arms. "No. You don't get to feel sorry. Not for this. Do you understand me?" I shake my head that's buried in her chest. "What happened to you was too much for anyone to go through, and I will never blame you for making the decision you made. I just wish you would have told me so I could have been there for you. It breaks my heart to know you had to carry this all alone. I'm your mother, I'm supposed to make things easier."

"You didn't see the way he looked at me yesterday momma. I can't see him again. Not after that. Whatever we thought we could be was quickly taken away yesterday when once again my past came back to haunt me."

She walks over and picks my suitcase up off my bed, setting it down on the floor between us. "Okay. Then I guess we should get on the road. You have a plane to catch."

I look around my bedroom one last time before walking out and shutting the door behind me. Today I just need to get back to my apartment in the city, where I can spend the rest of the night crying, until I run out of tears.

But tomorrow. Tomorrow I have to suck it up and move on with my life. I've spent the last twelve years without Graham Thomas, I just need to remember how to live without him again.

Epilogue

Lennox

A thirty minute drive to the first airport, followed by a small puddle jumper airplane to Detroit Metro, then a ridiculous three hour layover because they apparently double booked an airplane. How does that even happen? All of this plus the two hour flight into New York, and crazy traffic, led to an exhausted Lennox finally walking up to the door of my apartment.

Home. I try to feel relieved that I'm back, and that the sound of the traffic and horns outside is calming compared to the eerie silence of the small town I just left behind. But it's all a lie. I never realized how much I missed Iron City until I was walking away from it twelve years after I left the first time.

I dig my keys out of my purse and unlock the door, pulling my suitcase in behind me. "Shit." I mumble when I notice the small dead house plant that sits on the table in the entryway. I've had that damn thing for six years, it's basically been my most stable relationship here in the city.

I leave my suitcase in the hallway and kick off my shoes by the door. I am in serious need of a drink, or ten after the last couple of days I've had.

Without flipping on the lights I walk past the living room and head directly for the wine fridge in the kitchen. "You should probably find a better place to put your hide-a-key than underneath the welcome mat." The voice I've longed to hear all day makes me jump. I walk into the living room and flip the light switch on.

"Jesus, Graham!" He is sitting directly across the room from the archway I'm standing under that separates the living room and dining room. "What the hell are you doing here?"

He smiles. "You were right."

Confused by what he's talking about I cross my arms across my chest, "Right about what?"

"You really can't see the stars at all here. I've been sitting in this chair, just looking out the window for over an hour waiting for you and I don't think I can see a single damn star in the sky." I don't speak, instead I just stare at him in disbelief and he continues. "Remember that night, after you girls went out, and we ended up at the baseball fields? You told me when you were laying in the bed of the truck, how much you missed looking at the stars. And you're right, you can't see them here. Reason number three why you should move back to Michigan."

"Oh yeah, and what's reason number one and two?"

He stands up, and begins to make his way towards me. "That's simple. Two is your mom. I could see it in her eyes today, just how badly she wanted you back near her."

My voice stutters, "You went to see my momma?"

"Of course. How else would I have gotten this?" He pulls the ring that has had a home on my moms left hand for the past thirty-plus years out of his pocket.

My breath hitches as all the possibilities of why Graham is holding the engagement ring my dad gave my mom when he asked her to spend the rest of her life with him.

"Why - "

He places a feather light kiss to my lips before I get my question out. "And that brings us to reason number one." Graham drops down to his knee in front of me, "Lennox Coleman you have this way of running when things get tough between us. But this time I'm not letting you run. I want you, all of you and if that means I have to move to this damn city, then I will do it because I love you. I've always loved you. I know the way I reacted the other morning was not how it should have gone down. And I'm sorry. I'm definitely not perfect, and we have a lot to talk about and time to make up for, but I can't imagine spending another day without you Lenny. You are my forever girl."

I stare at him, tears in my eyes and hands shaking while I try to figure out what to say. "You forgot to mention reason number one." A small smile escapes my lips.

"Me. Better yet, us." He pulls my hand closer to him, "What do you say sweet lips, marry me?"

An unexpected giggle falls out of me as the dam holding everything back explodes. "Yes, but under one condition."

He starts to place the antique oval shaped diamond onto my finger and stops midway. "Anything, name it."

"You have to take my last name."

Lord, if I could have a picture of this man's face as he tries to digest the words that just came out of my mouth. "Ah, I mean, if that's - "

"I'm just kidding. Yes I'll marry you. My one condition is that we move home. Let's go back to Iron City."

He slides the ring that holds such significance onto my finger and then stands up, pulling me into my arms along the way. "I'm so sorry Lenny. I never should've made you leave yesterday. I was so messed up in my head and I was mostly worried about saying something I didn't mean. I never imagined when I got to your house today, that your mom was going to tell me she already took you to the airport."

"I wanted to come see you, but I was worried that you would still be angry and I couldn't handle it. I thought it was best to walk away, but I promise I won't ever walk away from you again Graham."

His lips crash down on mine, but he suddenly pulls away. "I have one condition to us getting married as well."

I take his lead and repeat what he just said to me moments ago. "Anything, name it."

"Marry me tomorrow." The words come out more like a statement than a question.

"Are you crazy? Your mom will have your tail if she finds out you got married and they weren't there."

He slowly backs me up to the wall and places both hands on either side of my head. "I don't care. We can have a reception or hell, a whole other wedding back home if that will make you happy. But tonight, I want to try and beat our one night orgasm record and tomorrow - tomorrow I want to make you my wife."

"Deal."

He picks me up, throwing my upper body over his shoulder, then grunts out the word "bedroom." After I point him in the direction of my room, he slaps my butt playfully causing me to giggle.

How did I ever think for one second I could walk away from this man and still be more than a shell of the woman that I am when I'm with him?

Graham

This is the second time in a month that I've had the title of "The Groom". Only this time, there's no little voice in the back of my head asking me if I'm making the right choice. There's really never been another choice besides Lennox. There isn't another woman who owns my heart that I'm walking away from. Instead, the girl I used to dream about marrying will be the woman walking toward me today in a simple white dress she found at a thrift shop down the road earlier.

After I followed through on my promise last night of giving her more than four orgasms, she fell asleep, exhausted from her day of travel. I laid next to her until I was sure she was out, and then kissed her on the forehead before heading to the kitchen to start making calls. She might have thought I was joking about getting married the following day but I've never been more serious in my life.

Five calls, reserving another private plane and here we are, in the mountains just outside of upstate New York. I try not to ever throw my family's money around, it's just not how we were brought up. Dad always says "As a Thomas you work your ass off to get what you want and when all else fails you, there's isn't much out there that money can't buy." So that's exactly what I did. Called in a few favors to get us to this small venue overlooking some of the most beautiful mountains I've ever seen in all my years of travel.

"You ready Graham?" The short, round chaplin pats me on the shoulder, informing me that it's time.

"I've never been more ready for anything in my life." And just as the words leave my lips, Lennox walks around the corner, in the thrift shop dress that hugs her perfect curves, hair piled on top of her head with loose curls flowing out around her face. And that dimple. God I'm a lucky man, I get to see that dimple for as long as I'm breathing.

The view behind us has nothing on the view I'm staring at right now. Lennox Coleman is a dream, my forever girl. Someone I never expected to walk back into my life the way she did.

But I guess fate has a way of doing that, bringing people back to you at just the right time.

What's that saying?

If you love something, you set it free… with the hope that someday, it'll come back to you.

The End

See you around… *hearts*

Acknowledgments

Sigh

Someone pinch me because this all still feels like a dream.

This book was hard for me - so hard. And there were so many times that I wanted to throw my laptop out the window and give up. So a special thank you to my best friend Arika Rae, because you talked me off the ledge more times than I can count. You took the first half of this book and stayed up all night reading it because I needed you to tell me if I was wasting my time or not. Instead of waking up to a "it sucks, you should probably just throw in the towel and give up" text, I woke to you telling me how in love you are with these characters and to keep going because it will be so worth it. And it was. Appreciation isn't a big enough word. Graham and Lenny would've never seen the light of day without you.

So many people have a hand in my writing process...

Beau. Sometimes you come home to a still messy house on my day off, only to find me sitting behind my laptop. And yet, instead of being angry about the piles of untouched laundry or dishes in the sink, you walk in, kiss me and ask how the writing's going. That's one of the many reasons I love you. Your understanding and support on this journey continues to mean the world to me.

My girls. These women put up with so much. I don't know how many times over the past year they've helped with cover design, picking out names, proofreading, and so much more. And most of the time it's at crazy hours of the night. They're literally the best team of badasses a writer could ask for and I'm forever grateful for them.

My fantastic editors - Lori, you are a gift. I swear, sometimes I think you believe in my talent and dreams even more than I do. I am so thankful for everything you do, and how quickly and efficiently you do it. And Alek, you took one look at my timeline and instead of laughing you said "We got this" and made magic happen. I appreciate you and am grateful to have a male point of view in the editing process.

Shout out to the endless support I get from my parents and family.

A special thank you to close friends of mine who allowed me to take a part of their fairytale romance and put it on paper for Graham and Lennox's story.

You. The readers. None of this would be possible without you. I think the best thing about this journey is when I receive messages from complete strangers telling me how my words made them cry, laugh or even scream. And what makes my inner nerd come out and my heart swell is when people tell me how my books have helped them fall in love with reading again.

Everyone has a happy place. Somewhere you go when you just need a break from reality and to escape life for awhile. Mine is located at the inside of a book, and I hope everyone reading this was able to find an escape for a few hours inside these pages.

Thank you for the support and I hope you fall in love with Graham and Lennox, their unwavering love and struggles as much as I did. Next up, JR. And I can honestly say, I'm ready for a break from the seriousness this book brought and I'm excited to jump into the crazy,

fun and passionate world of JR, Charlie & sweet
little Tucker.

XO, Brit

Graham & Lennox's Playlist

Chasin' You - Morgan Wallen
Fight Song - Rachel Platten
Why Ya Wanna - Jana Kramer
Home - Daughtry
The One That Got Away - Jake Owen
I Hold On - Dierks Bentley
Not Over You - Gavin Degraw
Hide The Wine - Carly Pearce
It's Not Over - Daughtry
We Were Us - Keith Urban & Miranda Lambert
Lips Of An Angel - Hinder
Babe - Sugarland ft. Taylor Swift (Emma's song)
3 AM - Matchbox Twenty
Drops Of Jupiter - Train
Bright Lights - Matchbox Twenty
Good As You - Kane Brown
Bed Of My Chevy - Justin Moore
Lettin' The Night Roll - Justin Moore
Famous In A Small Town - Miranda Lambert
Speechless - Dan + Shay

Iron City Heat Series

Someone Like You
(Walker & Quinn)

Someone Like Me
(Luke & Halee)

Someone Like Her
(Graham & Lennox)

Coming Soon:

Someone Like Him
(JR & Charlie)

Connect with Brit.

Instagram:
Instagram.com/Brit_Huyck
Facebook:
facebook.com/authorbrithuyck
Facebook Reader Group:
Brits Book Babes
Goodreads:
goodreads.com/author/Brittni_Huyck

Turn the page for a sneak peek of....

Someone
Like
Him

Chapter 1

Charlie

It's nine o'clock on a Saturday night. I have a glass of my favorite Pinot Grigio sitting on the table next to me, the little man in my life is sweetly tucked away in his bed, I just opened to the first page of my favorite authors new book, and my feet are draped across the gorgeous man sitting on the other end of my sectional.

Life is good.

Oh but wait, did I forget to mention that the completely intoxicating six-foot-two man has an unfair amount of perfectly defined muscles, and a square jaw that is lightly dusted with stubble that's described in all of my romance novels... yeah that guy. The type of man that women dream about because he's not only extremely easy on the eyes, but he also can make me laugh like no one has ever been able to before and he's so, so sweet. I often find myself wondering if he is even real. But he's real, so deliciously real. And he's my best friend.

So ask me why I have Jameson Ryan Hunter, this perfect specimen of a man, stuck in the friend zone?

That question is easy to answer.

One Word. Trey.

My ex-husband who became a drunk and slowly forced me to lose all hope in men. Trey wasn't always a bad guy. In fact, when we met and the year following he seemed just as perfect as my best friend sitting next to me whose attention is fully focused on whether or not his pick of the two rival college football teams playing, will win.

But after having Tucker, our son, and all the stresses and pressures that come along with working full time at his father's consulting company and going to school full time to get his masters, so he could one day take over the company, something in Trey snapped. It started slow, like I would assume most alcoholics start. A few beers at the end of the night to help cope with the weight of the day. But over time a few beers in the evening turned into sneaking alcohol in his coffee mug in the morning and taking a few shots at lunch. He eventually became someone who didn't even resemble the man I fell in love with. A once calm and loving soul became easily angry at the most ridiculous things.

Which is basically what led me here, to Iron City. One night, after a long, grueling, twelve hour day at the salon, I drove over and picked up Tuck from my parents, because apparently Trey was just too exhausted to stop and grab him on his way home. I was already frustrated when we finally pulled into the driveway at the idea of it being after eight and I still needed to bathe Tucker and get him in bed when this could have been done already if my husband would just step up to the plate a little more these days. But when I walked in to find the coffee table covered in beer cans and a half empty fifth of vodka grasped in his drunken, passed out hands, I thought the anger inside of me might actually explode. Needless to say, there was more screaming than I was comfortable with in front of our two-year-old and when he reached over, forcefully trying to yank him out of my arms to *give him a bath,* something inside me snapped.

And I was done.

I started packing bags to leave, which just seemed to set him off more. Eventually I had to call the police because I was concerned he was going to end up hurting me or even worse our little boy. While the police asked him to come down to the station for questioning and to sober up, I left. I fled to the last place I remembered feeling the safest.

Which was Iron City. My parents and grandparents used to bring me up here in the summers and we would rent houses on the various lakes that surrounded the small Michigan town.

"What's going through your head, beautiful?" The fog of my past drifts away as my eyes find JR's.

"Oh, nothing."

"It sure didn't look like nothing. You opened that book at least ten minutes ago, but haven't turned a page since. That's typically what happens when I open books, but not you." I smile at his words. Since the first time he saw me, quietly reading a book in the corner chair at the salon while Halee cut his hair, he's picked on me since, about being a nerd. He shifts his body so more weight is on his left hip, turning his hard, defined, shirt covered torso so it's facing me. "Tell me where you went just then. Maybe I can help."

What my best friend doesn't realize is that he does help. After that first time we met, Jameson walked into my life and even more importantly, Tucker's, and hasn't left. Sometimes I find myself wishing it was a different world and the twenty-year old version of myself met JR first, then maybe I wouldn't be like I am now. A woman who is hesitant to let any man back in. But whenever my mind travels down that dark path I try to remind myself that even though Trey didn't turn out to be the man I hoped I would grow old with, I still got my sweet little guy because of him. And Tucker alone is enough of a reason to deal with the crappy hand I've been dealing with the past few years.

"There you go again Charlie. What's up with you tonight? It's almost like you are living in a completely different world than me."

I smile, closing my book and setting it on the table next to my wine I have yet to touch. "Sorry. It's just been a long week, I know I'm not much fun tonight. If you have somewhere else you would rather be, I completely understand."

He pulls my feet closer, slides my socks off and starts massaging the soles of my achy, tired feet. His sincere and loving eyes find mine again before he answers, "There isn't anywhere else I would rather be."

"Why?" The question comes out of my mouth before I have a chance to stop it. "I mean, you're single and it's a Saturday night, why wouldn't you want to be out at the bar with all of your friends?"

"You're my friend."

"I know-" A sigh escapes my lips. "But you know what I mean."

His fingers stop the circular motion they were just doing and he looks at me straight in the eyes. "Listen, we go over this every time I'm here with you. I'm here because I want to be here, because I enjoy spending time with you, and spending time with Tuck. If I wanted to be at the bar, I would be. Simple as that. And for the record, *all of my friends* aren't at the bar anymore either. Walker is wifed up and knowing them, they're on round four or five of their crazy sexapades already tonight. Luke just got back from a week in Chicago for press stuff wrapping up his last tour, so I'm sure he's curled up on the couch with his girls. Graham and Lenny just took off for a couple week honeymoon in the mountains out west. So that leaves Will and Mack, who these days spend enough time at the bar to find their next conquest and then they are gone. And just for shits and giggles, let's say all of those assholes were at the bar tonight, I would still be sitting right here, with your cute little feet propped up on me, watching football. At some point you are going to get it through that incredibly thick, but beautiful head of yours that I actually enjoy quiet nights like this with you. I enjoy being *with* you in general. Okay?"

Suddenly feeling shy, I whisper "Okay."

"Okay." He says again, then turns himself so his attention is back on the game in front of him. All while his hands continue rubbing my feet again.

This is a conversation we have a lot. As always, I try and push him away, worried that if I don't keep him at arms length, I will actually let him in. And as per usual, he goes on one of his rants about how much I mean to him and that I'm not holding him back from anything.

So again, the question that always seems to resurface… why do I continue to keep Jameson Ryan Hunter in the friend zone?

To Be Continued…

Made in the USA
Lexington, KY
27 November 2019